THE GHOST NETWORK

ACTIVATE

Published by arrangement with Ferly.

Andrews McMeel Publishing
a division of Andrews McMeel Universal
1130 Walnut Street, Kansas City, Missouri 64106

www.andrewsmcmeel.com

19 20 21 22 23 SDB 10 9 8 7 6 5 4 3 2 1
Paperback ISBN: 978-1-4494-9711-8
Hardback ISBN: 978-1-5248-5164-4
Library of Congress Control Number: 2018955953

Made by:
Shenzhen Donnelley Printing Company Ltd.
Address and location of manufacturer:
No. 47, Wuhe Nan Road, Bantian Ind. Zone,
Shenzhen China, 518129
1st Printing—1/21/19

Editor: Jean Lucas
Designer: Tanja Kivistö
Art Director: Spencer Williams
Production Manager: Chuck Harper
Production Editor: Amy Strassner

ATTENTION: SCHOOLS AND BUSINESSES
Andrews McMeel books are available at quantity discounts with bulk purchase
for educational, business, or sales promotional use. For information,
please e-mail the Andrews McMeel Publishing Special Sales Department:
specialsales@amuniversal.com.

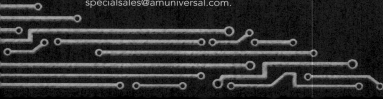

THE GHOST NETWORK

ACTIVATE

I. I. DAVIDSON

Andrews McMeel
PUBLISHING®

RUSSIA

Wales
Nome

Big Diomede

Diomede City

WOLF'S DEN

Little Diomede

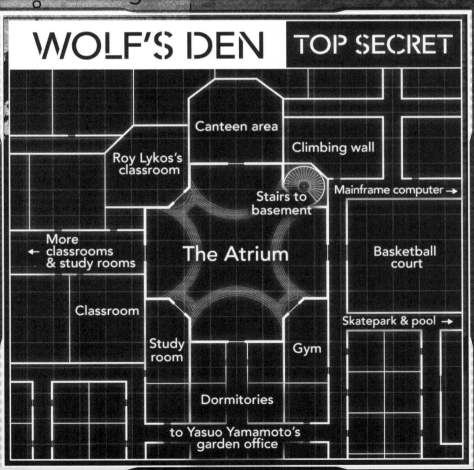

UNITED STATES

ALASKA

Fairbanks

CANADA

Anchorage

WOLF'S DEN TOP SECRET

Canteen area

Climbing wall

Roy Lykos's classroom

Stairs to basement

Mainframe computer →

← More classrooms & study rooms

The Atrium

Basketball court

Classroom

Skatepark & pool →

Study room

Gym

Dormitories

to Yasuo Yamamoto's garden office

Downloading...

Akane Maezono inched her toes out over the vertical
drop. She couldn't even *see* the ground.

And that's just how she liked it.

Above her, the night sky was piercingly black, with just a
scattering of stars. And even though she knew a two-thousand-
foot skyscraper didn't bring her closer to them, it certainly felt
that way. Up here on the roof, the night seemed darker, the air
so much clearer. The wind that engulfed her was cold enough to
sharpen her brain with icy clarity. Sprawled out below her were
the bright lights of Tokyo. She gazed at the office windows and
pitied the salaried workers who stayed late and dutifully at their
desks. The sea of red brake lights made it seem like half the
population was paralyzed in traffic. *I don't have those problems.*
Akane grinned in sheer delight and clutched the straps of her
BASE chute.

The drop site was a fairly broad alley behind the building,
but it was barely lit. It had to be that way, but she'd scoped it out
before in careful detail. She knew exactly where she had to land,

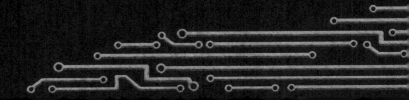

and she'd be out of there before police and building security knew what had hit them.

Her heart was racing, and her veins were surging with adrenaline. *Two thousand feet to the ground. This is going to be* awesome.

Taking a deep breath of the crisp air, she prepared herself to leap—

The piercing alarm on her phone earpiece startled her.

She stumbled backward, and her feet slipped back onto the roof. Blood surged through her veins even more at the shock of the interruption. She quickly pressed the button by her ear.

"Who's this?"

"Akane, get out of there."

She was silent for a moment, breathing hard. "What the—who is this?"

"It's John. I don't have time to explain. You're busted!"

"John?" John whom she'd never actually met? John her fellow hacker who lived in *Vancouver*? "John *Laine*?"

"Get out of there!"

"No!" she snapped. Half angry, half curious, she asked, "What are you talking about, John Laine?"

With a long, impatient sigh, he said, "Building security's onto you. They've called the cops!"

Shoot. She glanced around anxiously, half expecting the entire metropolitan police department to come dashing across the roof. "How do you know?"

"It doesn't matter! Look, just run and I'll explain later."

"How did you even know where I was? I'm totally psyched up for this jump—"

"And you'll blow it."

<8>

"Yes, I would now, because you've freaked me out!" Cursing, Akane ran for the stairwell.

"*And* they're bringing cars up the alley, which will ruin your drop site."

Point taken. She gripped the door handle but paused, scowling. "I'm out of here. *As soon as you explain yourself.*"

She heard him exhale with frustration. "Great plans, Akane. Lots of detail. Awesome preparation. I hacked them."

"You couldn't have! They were on my own secure server! You needed a special download to break the code."

"Well, I guess I downloaded it."

"*You. Couldn't. Have.*" He really couldn't have. She was a way better hacker than he was. What was more, she knew every detail of *his* system, and his hardware didn't have the capacity—

"I was worried, so I tracked you. Akane, if you want the truth, I don't know *how* I cracked that code. The download started automatically. Sheer luck, I guess. The rest was easy—I hacked the building's security system, and I hacked the police radio. *Is this enough information* to convince you *to get out of there?*"

It certainly was. It was just as well she'd hacked the building's security and layout herself, or she wouldn't have known about the alternate exit routes. As she let the stairwell door slam behind her—cutting off the coolness of the breeze and the stars—she was already running, tears of disappointment stinging her eyes.

She wiped them away, annoyed. *Dang it, John Laine*—

He'd done the right thing. Her feet pounded down the stairs. He'd acted as her virtual ground crew without her even knowing it, and he'd *done the right thing.*

<9>

But as she ducked into the fire escape and bolted down the stairs, two at a time, she could hardly decide whether she was grateful or angry. Even the hot buzz of frustrated adrenaline was overpowered by her utter disbelief.

John Laine could not have hacked my plans. I know what he can do on a computer, and he's not capable. He had no way of accessing that code. It did NOT start downloading automatically.

And friend, fellow hacker, or not, she was going to get to the bottom of this. Because there was only one thing she knew right now, and she knew it with absolute certainty.

HE COULD NOT HAVE DOWNLOADED THAT KEY.

<10>

One

"Stop it, John. I can't breathe." Jake Hook was over-come with laughter, his usually pale face bright red because of his struggle to stay quiet. "Nah, I don't mean it. Do it again!"

John Laine grinned at his co-conspirator, waving his hand to shush him. Any minute now, the boy was actually going to *explode.* "Mrs. Long is gonna kill us, Jake."

"Only if she c-catches us." A huge snort of laughter escaped. "And quit calling me *Jake.* You know by now my name is Slack. Quick, she's coming again!"

The two of them were huddled behind a parked pickup truck and peering over its hood at the doors of Bentley Mall. Slack had his phone propped against the truck's side mirror, with the camera running.

He should have been getting good footage; John could see their school principal quite clearly.

The poor woman decided to have another go at leaving the mall. With her jaw clenched, she marched toward the doors, swinging her shopping bags like she planned to barge straight through the glass if they *dared* close on her again.

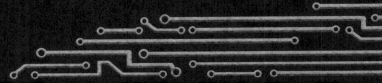

John waited, counting in his head, then tapped his own phone screen as the doors slid shut. This time, Mrs. Long was so close she nearly bumped her nose on the glass. She staggered back and actually *yelled* at the doors.

Slack fell over backward laughing and smacked his head on the Chevy's fender, but this didn't sober him up at all. Rubbing his head, he quickly scrambled forward again, with tears running down his cheeks. "She backed up. *Open them!*"

"We should stop," John said, starting to feel guilty. "What if she's got an important appointment or something?"

"If the dragon's got an appointment, it's with some poor kid for detention." Slack peered eagerly over the truck's hood and raised his phone. "No mercy, John!"

Slack had a point. Anyway, this was the best hack yet, so they should make the most of it. John's finger hovered over his screen as Mrs. Long glared at the sliding doors. She took another two steps back.

He opened them.

She didn't scream or yell this time. In fact she almost caught him off guard by sprinting forward to break free. In just the nick of time, he jabbed the screen with his finger, and the doors closed. Mrs. Long twisted just enough, but her shoulder collided with the glass and she bounced back, dropping both bags.

"Are you even getting this?" John peered doubtfully at Slack, who had collapsed against his arm, his messy blond hair obscuring John's screen.

"Enough," gasped Slack, getting control of himself to check the camera. "Anyway, I can edit it. This is going to get *epic* views."

<12>

John peered over the truck again, and his eyes widened. "Hey, she's got the security guard. Time to go!"

Half dragging the giggling Slack, he crawled around the truck and between another two cars. Lifting his head, he peered back at the mall entrance. Mrs. Long was pointing at the doors and explaining something in *very* animated terms to the perplexed guard.

"Wait!" he whispered. Frantically, he tapped his phone screen again, canceling the hack. As the security guard walked hesitantly forward, the doors slid obediently open.

The guard turned to Mrs. Long and spread out his arms in a disbelieving shrug.

"Cracking me uuuppp," hiccuped Slack, wiping his eyes as he lowered his phone. "I got that too. Let's get out of here!"

The two boys ran hunched over between the cars and bolted across College Road. The angry blare of a car horn followed them as they dived into the trees on the other side. They kept running, following the sluggish brown water of the stream till they were safely under the iron railway bridge. John staggered to a halt, panting.

Slack was way behind, but when he caught up, John knew what had slowed him down: he was still laughing. "That was the best one yet!"

"Better than filming Mr. Brewster picking his nose in the elevator?" John grinned.

"Way better." Slack wrinkled his nose in deep thought. "Maybe just about equal to Madison Harper squeezing that zit before she took a selfie."

"I still feel kinda bad about that one."

<13>

"Don't," Slack ordered him. "She's the vainest, meanest Mean Girl in junior high. She'd do it to someone else in a heartbeat."

"If she was smart enough to hack a phone," agreed John, and they both collapsed in giggles again.

The summer heat of Fairbanks had truly passed, and the September breeze that whistled under the bridge had an air of coolness. John was still hot and sweating from their run. Stripping off his jacket, he flopped back into the scraggly grass and closed his eyes. His online life had always been interesting—much more interesting than daily life in Fairbanks, Alaska, or in Vancouver before that—but with Slack around, it was a *lot* more fun.

OK, he'd always thought of himself as a good guy, a white-hat hacker, and most of the time John was still that. Helping out the victims of online hoaxes went a long way toward making up for an occasional prank video, like the one they'd just taken of Mrs. Long. Besides, he'd brought Slack over from the dark side, hadn't he? Before the two of them had met, Slack's hacking adventures had served mostly to fill his room with more expensive electronic equipment than any thirteen-year-old should own—all purchased with fake gift cards and stolen credit card details.

But after that, when Slack had hacked John's phone to track him and then John had hacked him right back in revenge, they'd discovered that they had a lot more in common than they thought. John had suddenly gained a new friend in real life—his first since he and his mother and sister had moved north from Vancouver. And Slack had been wildly excited at the idea of joining John and his online friends in their hoax-hunting group, the White Eyes.

John still felt a little twinge of guilt for making Mrs. Long look so ridiculous by hacking the mall door controls. But hey, he

<14>

reasoned, the pranks that Slack thought up were pretty harmless. It was kind of like being a trickster—like Loki, and wasn't Loki his favorite character in the Norse myths he loved? Loki was OK—well, when he wasn't killing people and wreaking havoc. And anyway, it had been a *long* time since John had laughed this much.

Not since his father's disappearance, in fact.

"Hey." Slack's voice interrupted his thoughts at exactly the right moment, just before they got too dark. "How's your sister?"

John ripped up a handful of grass and threw it at him. "She's as big a pain as ever. Don't get your hopes up. Leona thinks computer geeks are *lame*."

"Also, she's too old for me," sighed Slack, rolling onto his side and propping his head dreamily on one hand. "Don't say it."

"I wasn't going to, but she is! She's sixteen, and she's really, really boring. When she isn't being annoying."

"One day she'll appreciate me," sniffed Slack, tossing his hair. "She's a sophisticated city girl, and she'll take a while to recognize the fine, down-to-earth qualities of a northern boy is all. And she's not boring, by the way. She drives your grandpa's snowmobile like a *demon*."

John rolled his eyes. "Well, at least she got the two of us together, so she's useful for something."

"Yeah," said Slack. "If Leona hadn't told me you were your momma's precious baby since your dumb accident . . . "

" . . . your own sister wouldn't have told Leona exactly the same about you," John finished for him, and they both started to laugh again.

When Slack had decided to hack John's phone, it had been as a kind of twisted revenge for that breach of secrecy by Slack's

<15>

sister, Nina. Slack couldn't have foreseen that it was never going to work: John was always on the alert for hostile phone hacks, since his father had constantly drummed the dangers into his head.

But John was glad now that Slack had made the attempt. It was pretty strange that they'd both had serious accidents before they even started school, but it was just one more thing he and Slack had in common. He hadn't thought he needed a friend in Fairbanks—after all, he could talk to his best friend, Akane, in Tokyo with the swipe of a touchpad. So he'd kept to himself when his family first moved to Fairbanks, and he'd probably gotten a reputation for being moody and unfriendly. But meeting Slack had changed everything in a few short weeks.

Still, thinking about Akane had reminded him, so he scrambled to his feet and brushed the grass off his torn jeans. "I need to get back," he told Slack. "I told Akane I'd talk to her this morning."

Slack glanced at his phone. "You're way late."

"I mean this morning for her. It's 9 a.m. in Tokyo."

"Huh. Fun's over, I guess."

"Except that you want to join the White Eyes, right?" Suddenly nervous, John raked back his long black hair with his fingers. "Why don't you come back with me and we can talk to Akane together?"

Slack leaped to his feet, his ice-blue eyes flashing with his broad grin.

"Sure! Especially if your sister's going to be there . . . "

<16>

Two

Was Obaasan *ever* going to go out? Akane rested her chin on the windowsill and stared out at the blossom-less cherry trees. The beautiful view of Gotenyama Garden might be all her grandmother needed for entertainment, but Akane was bored. Her father was at work, her mother was at the supermarket, and her three perfect sisters were allowed to go out, of course. And she was stuck here inside with Obaasan, who, given her love of gossip, seemed to be taking an extraordinarily long time to get ready for her daily trip to the market.

OK, her current situation *might* have something to do with yesterday's exploits, but it had been a whole sixteen hours since the cops had caught her on top of the Mori Tower at the Torano-mon Hills complex. Her luck had to run out sometime—espe-cially since a year ago she'd warned John Laine, repeatedly, *never* to hack her projects again—and yesterday had been the day.

Akane had gone out of her way to wash the rice dishes and miso soup bowls from breakfast. Surely, she'd made up for her mishap already. Didn't her grandmother trust her anymore?

She hadn't even been BASE jumping—this time. Sure, she'd been taking photographs, and the climbing gear and the BASE chute on her back had taken some explaining, but no harm done. And even if she'd jumped, there'd *still* have been no harm done, because it wasn't like she was some *amateur*.

And now, in more than one sense, she was grounded. Akane sighed.

"*Mata ne*, Akane." Obaasan's voice behind her contained a distinct note of warning. She was pulling on her favorite yellow coat. "See you soon. I won't be long."

"*Jya ne*, Obaasan." Akane tried to give her grandma a quick smile as she left, though she could hardly contain her impatience. As soon as the door of the apartment clicked shut, she darted to her computer and turned it on.

And there was John, waiting for her in the window in the corner of her screen, looking anxious and almost as impatient as she was. She let out a sigh of relief.

"Hey, I thought I'd missed you." He grinned. Akane clicked to enlarge him, and his rugged face filled the screen. She casually greeted him, "*Ohayo*, John! How's it going with that doofus who thought he could hack you?"

"Uhh . . . " John's eyes shifted to the side with a sudden awkwardness, and someone shoved him aside. Another face peered at her: ice-blue eyes, tangled blond hair, and an indignant smirk.

"The doofus is right here," said the new arrival. His scowl faded as he stared at Akane, and his eyes widened.

Akane peered back at him, unrepentant. "Well, the doofus ought to have known better than to try to hack John Laine," she

<18>

pointed out sternly. "Not only is he wise to that, but also he's got friends who will notice if he doesn't."

"Well, *konnichiwaaa*," drawled the blond, donning what he obviously thought was a charming grin. "Hey, are you telling me it was you who tipped John off?"

Akane glanced at the two faces who were now competing for screen space. John was grimacing in embarrassment. "I mentioned it, but he already knew," she lied. "And we don't say '*konnichiwa*' at this hour of the morning."

"It's after four in Fairbanks," said the boy, with an easy shrug. "Hey, I'm Slack."

"That's your name, or you're just a slacker?" She sat back and folded her arms. There was something *really* irritating about this kid. At least John was smart and streetwise enough not to be led astray. *At least I hope he is*, she thought, narrowing her eyes.

She had felt protective of John ever since she'd gotten to know him better—and since she'd learned of his past. It was true that he was super cautious about his computer and his phone, and even if he hadn't been so focused and serious *and* even if he wasn't one of the best hackers she knew, his father would have made sure he was on guard.

Mikael Laine had been one of the most skilled brain surgeons in the world—but sometimes even the fastest and the best don't have time to save all the people who need them. This was why he'd been so paranoid about desperate people taking desperate measures to access his skills—even perhaps tracking his kids and kidnapping them. And maybe this sounded far-fetched, thought Akane, but at thirteen years old she'd seen enough in her hacking

<19>

career to know just how far people would go when they wanted something badly enough.

Mikael Laine had been absolutely right to be paranoid, in her opinion. And now that Mikael was missing—presumed dead—it was her responsibility to keep malicious people away from John.

Which was why, unbeknownst to John, she'd been tracking him for some time. The last thing she needed was some eager little noob finding out about this and telling John. She clenched her jaw and gave Slack a hostile glare.

John shoved his new friend aside. "Akane, listen. Slack really wants to join the White Eyes. What do you think?"

"He does?" He didn't strike her as the type. Akane wrinkled her nose skeptically. "Is he any good?"

John and Slack exchanged a grin. "Yeah," said John. "He's good."

Akane frowned, her instincts tingling. "You guys haven't been doing anything stupid, have you?"

"'Course not!" said John, a little too emphatically.

He pondered for a moment and then glanced at Slack. "OK, so he's been a bit of a bad guy in the past, right, Slack? But he's gotten bored with that. I'll vouch for his skills *and* his good intentions."

Akane sighed, looking from one boy to the other. She wasn't convinced by Slack's humble expression; she didn't know him.

But she knew John better than she knew her own sisters. He wasn't the type to jump when he couldn't see the ground—it was one thing she didn't have in common with him, she thought wryly, but she couldn't help admiring his sense of caution. The John she knew didn't rush into friendships without thinking.

<20>

He was so reserved he was almost aloof. She'd occasionally wanted to slap the computer screen and tell him that if he didn't come across as so arrogant, he might not be so lonely. And since his father's disappearance, she'd hated the sadness that hung over him. It hurt to see that, but it was difficult to help when she was half a world away.

But sadness was not what she was seeing in John's face right now. He didn't look reserved or aloof either. There was a spark of real happiness in his brown eyes. *He could use a friend. Somebody he could talk to without logging on . . .*

Akane rubbed at her birthmark. It was a long ridge of hard flesh under her hair at the back of her skull, and as much as her habit of scratching at it annoyed her sisters, it always helped her think.

At last, she nodded slowly.

"If you trust him, John, so do I. Let's give him a chance."

"You're in, Slack!" The boys exchanged a high five.

John looked delighted, but Akane couldn't repress the tremor of doubt in her spine. Maybe it was only a face on a computer screen, but there was something mischievous about Slack's blue eyes. Anarchic, even.

I hope I'm not going to regret this . . .

<21>

Three

"You haven't mentioned my sister once since we spoke to Akane," said John, nudging Slack with his elbow.

"Don't get me wrong." Slack was confidently strutting down the school corridor, his backpack slung casually over one shoulder. "Leona's a nice girl from a good family, but I'm sorry, John. Your sister and I are not to be. My heart belongs to Akane— what's her last name—Makono."

"*Maezono*," John corrected him, laughing. "Better get her name right if she's your true love."

Slack's cocky grin faded a little as they turned the corner and the principal's door came into view. He halted. "So what do you think Mrs. Long wants?"

John found his jubilant mood draining away. He swallowed. "Dunno. But she can't possibly know about . . . y'know. That. The doors."

"It'll be about our grades," said Slack, reassuring himself. "I actually *studied* for that last French quiz. She's gonna congratulate us. You'll see."

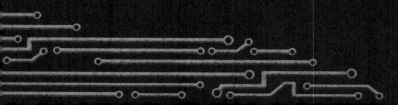

John was pretty sure that was not what was going to happen, but he said nothing as they trudged warily toward the office. He'd just raised his knuckles to rap on the door when it flew open.

"Gentlemen," said Mrs. Long, in that over-polite voice of hers that meant they were absolutely in for it. "Do come in . . ."

"John. Jake. I'm sure you both know what this is about." The principal had laced her fingers together and was peering at them over the rim of her glasses. "But to save you both the trouble of creating a fantastical story that would be embarrassing for all of us, let me show you something."

John's mouth felt dry as she swiveled her desktop screen toward them. Mrs. Long was taking her time; her eyes held a glint that told him she was enjoying this—a lot more than he or Slack was going to.

He swallowed hard as she clicked her mouse. Yes, that was their video she was running on YouTube. Beside him, Slack was now choking back his laughter; his lips were pressed tightly together, and his eyes were starting to water. John wanted to kick him, but that would be a dead giveaway.

He cleared his throat and said in an unintentionally high voice, "I don't, um—"

"Know anything about it? Of course you don't, Mr. Laine." With a severe glance, Mrs. Long clicked again.

The new video was definitely not one of his and Slack's. He knew because they were in it.

The phone footage was a little wobbly, but the identity of the two boys crouched behind the truck was perfectly clear.

<23>

Slack's phone was pointed toward the mall doors, though he kept almost dropping it in all the hilarity. John could see his own long, dark, straight hair and his prized flea-market leather jacket. As for Slack's warm-up jacket, that was an expensive one of a kind, and his distinctive hair straggled over the collar. The clincher came when they turned to one another and Mrs. Long froze the frame on their laughing profiles.

The two boys sat in silence. John didn't feel like Loki anymore; he felt like an idiot. Even Slack seemed to have lost the urge to giggle.

"Now," Mrs. Long leaned forward and clasped her hands, "I guess you can imagine that I'm not very pleased."

Slack stared at the desk. John swallowed hard. "Mrs. Long, I'm really sorry—" he began.

"I'm sure you are." She glared from one side to the other, from John to Slack, and then at her computer screen. "That's quite a few humiliating views."

"We'll take it down," said Slack quickly.

"I hope so. I hope you'll also take down the footage you hacked from Madison Harper's phone. Not very nice, boys, was it? And while I've been investigating your antics, I've discovered your neighbor Mr. Brewster isn't too pleased with you either."

John had no idea what to say. It was probably best to stay quiet.

"By the way, it was one of your own classmates who caught and filmed you. I'm not going to tell you who it was." Mrs. Long tapped her screen with a fingernail. "But perhaps you might reflect upon the fact that neither of you are *quite* as popular as you think you are."

"I don't—" blurted John.

<24>

"No, John, but perhaps you're not quite as *clever* as you think. And maybe, Jake, your pranks lose their appeal when you play them on a few too many people."

"Yes, Mrs. Long." Slack's pale face had turned a dark shade of red.

"Now, what to do with you?" The principal leaned back in her swivel chair with the air of a spider who couldn't decide between two juicy flies. "I have a feeling that suspension would just be playing into your hands. You clearly have more than enough spare time as it is. In your case, Jake, it's because you're not remotely interested in your schoolwork—but John, I'm disappointed in you.

"You were an outstanding scholar in Vancouver, and until the past few weeks, you've done very well here. I wonder what has changed?"

She was glaring at Slack, but it was John who felt the pit of shame in his stomach.

"However," Mrs. Long sat forward again and said, "I know things have been difficult for you, John, since . . . what happened with your father."

The shame subsided, and a familiar little knot of grief surfaced in John's chest.

"And I'll say this much for both of you," she went on. "You are very imaginative. And you're clearly talented. That's why it's taken me a few days to decide on an appropriate punishment." Her lips tightened. "This hacking skill you both have—I'm not going to say I approve of it, because I don't. But there has to be a way to—shall we say—turn it in a more positive direction."

"Go on." Slack had perked up again. At her razor-sharp stare, he gulped and added, "Um . . . please tell us more, Mrs. Long."

<25>

"I've spoken to your parents, Jake, and to John's mother, and we have all agreed that instead of getting the police involved"—she paused to let the real threat sink in—"a special education camp for a semester will do you both a world of good."

"Special education camp?" blurted John. *That sounds ominous.* "Isn't that a bit . . . extreme?"

For the first time, Mrs. Long actually laughed. "It sounds worse than it is, John. This is your first offense, after all. No, the only *extreme* part is the location. You'll both be going to Little Diomede."

"I've heard of that island." Slack's eyes narrowed. "There's nothing there!"

John's heart plummeted, and he thought he might be sick. *Extreme?* She wasn't kidding. "One tiny settlement," he said bleakly. "They can hardly even get deliveries, and that's when the weather's *good*. What are we supposed to do there, Mrs. Long? For a whole *semester?*"

Mrs. Long seemed to be enjoying herself more than ever. She pulled open a drawer with tantalizing slowness and set a file on the desk in front of her. Very delicately, she opened it and began to set papers on the desk, neatly, side by side. Judging from the gleam in her eyes, a big part of this punishment seemed to be telling them about it. John had seen friendlier movie sharks.

"What are you supposed to do there, John?" Her smile was broad. "You'd be surprised . . . "

<<>>

"Are you ever going to shut up about this?" Leona rolled her eyes and stabbed her fork at her burger. "Mom, tell him it's supposed to be a punishment."

<26>

John ignored his sister. "And it's not just advanced computer skills," he went on. "There's sports too. A skate park, a pool, and climbing walls. I don't know where they put it all—I mean, you should *see* Little Diomede Island on a map—"

"Sounds like I'm more than happy seeing it on a map," said Leona snarkily. "Suddenly, Fairbanks seems like a glittering metropolis."

"Leave him alone," laughed John's mother. "Yes, John, I know what's available. Mrs. Long showed me all the details. To be honest, I don't think it's much of a punishment either, but it'll do you a lot of good, I imagine. You've been cooped up with that computer of yours since we came to Fairbanks."

John sighed and lapsed into his best robotic voice. "John is the computer," he reminded her.

His mom, Tina, gave a rueful laugh. "I know, I know, but—"

"Hey, the computing's going to be the best part," protested John. "The Wolf's Den is only for the elite! The *best* technological students *in the world*." He glowered at Leona. "Which includes me, apparently, so take that."

"Yeah, 'cause John *is* the pain in the computer's butt."

"Hey!" Tina scolded. "Cut it out, both of you."

"You sure about this school, Tina?" John's grandfather, tapping the hot pads against his palm, turned from the stove. He'd just gotten home from tending the university's caribou herd, and his grizzled face was pink from the heat. "It's kind of remote."

"I wasn't sure to start with," admitted Tina. "But it sounds like the most secure place you can imagine, Dad. And I know 'John is the computer' was a joke between them, but Mikael always said

<27>

it wasn't far off." She looked sad for a moment. "John's special. A place like this could really boost his skills."

"Hmph," grunted Leona, her head down. "He's certainly special."

Her mother tapped her head lightly with a spoon. "Don't be jealous, honey. If you don't make a fuss, I'll take you on a shopping trip to Vancouver to compensate."

Leona brightened up instantly. "OK. Have a great time in the snowy wilderness, little brother! And don't fall off any rocks *again*."

Tina's eyes widened instantly with anxiety. "Yes, that's one thing. *Do* be careful, John."

"Mom, every kid at the school will be doing these sports."

"Well, you don't have to be the crazy guy. Leave that to your friend Jake." She kissed the top of his head, and he winced. "You know I worry."

Since she couldn't see his eyes, John rolled them. His mom certainly did worry. Of course, if he hadn't been dumb enough to fall and hit his head and nearly die, she wouldn't be so overprotective, but he'd only been five at the time.

Tina gave him a quick, tight hug. "Remember your dad's not around to save you again," she whispered. "Please be careful, John."

"I will, Mom," he muttered.

"Mom, chill," said Leona, ruffling John's hair in her annoying way. "He'll probably never go near a climbing wall. He'll be way too wrapped up in his computing stuff."

"A bit of fresh air would do him some good," grunted their grandfather, half under his breath.

"Pfft!" Leona waved her fork dismissively. "There's no *way* John'll do anything dangerous!"

<28>

Four

"This is worse than I thought." Slack was staring wide-eyed from the helicopter window as the craft swayed and lurched in the north wind. Clinging to the edge, his knuckles were white.

"They do this all the time," said John, trying to sound confident. "It's not like they haven't landed a helicopter here before."

"Who's talking about the helicopter?" said Slack glumly. "I mean the school. I thought it was going to be exciting."

John leaned across him to peer out. *What school?* was his first thought.

Little Diomede Island looked tiny from the air. It was shaped like one of his mom's less successful meat loaves: sheer sides that plummeted into a foaming ocean and a broad, flat plateau, as if some giant had sliced off its mountaintop with a knife. The plateau was bare except for a dusting of early snow, and as the helicopter dipped, John caught sight of the only buildings: a cluster of houses tucked around a peninsula.

Swimming pool? Climbing wall? The island looked like it barely had electricity.

"That'll be Diomede City," he remarked gloomily, pointing at the houses.

"City," echoed Slack, with a dismal face. "You think Mrs. Long pranked us back?"

John couldn't answer; the helicopter gave a sudden, violent lurch, and he clung tightly to his seat.

"Going down," yelled the pilot cheerfully.

For a moment John thought that was some ominous warning. His heart was pounding so hard he barely heard the rattle of the rotors, let alone Slack's yelp of delight. Only when his friend tugged on his sleeve did he finally gulp hard and lean across to look.

Below them, the icy ground was moving. John blinked. No, it wasn't just the motion of the aircraft. A whole section of the island's rocky surface was sliding back, vanishing smoothly under the rest of the plateau.

Dislodged snow tumbled down onto a compact helipad, and the helicopter swayed, lowered, and finally settled, its rotors slowing.

"Welcome to the Wolf's Den!" called the pilot, his grin making it obvious that he loved spooking his passengers.

John's legs were still trembling as he climbed down onto the helipad, and his fingers gripped his bag a little too tightly. When Slack slapped his back, he almost jumped out of his skin.

"This is *awesome!*" yelled his friend.

"It is," said John with a slow grin. "The school's under the surface!"

Not only had the helipad been revealed as the plateau slid away but also there was a vast glass roof beyond it to the north.

<30>

Beneath that, John could make out steel walkways, a cavernous, light-filled hall, and figures moving purposefully around. And that was only the limited section he could see.

He turned, orienting himself. Clouds scattered across the sky, but there were enough patches of sunshine to make the heaving sea sparkle. Wind tugged at his hair, whipping it across his eyes, and the cold air tasted sharp and clear. Slack gripped his arm and pointed across the expanse of sea.

"Another island," he shouted.

John was glad to have a chance to reassert himself; he was pretty sure Slack wouldn't have done any research. "That's Big Diomede. Belongs to Russia. It's across the dateline. It's already tomorrow there!"

"Whoa. Maybe there's another school out there. Or an annex to this one?"

"Nah, it's uninhabited." John couldn't help feeling smug.

Slack gave him a withering look and pointed at the gigantic complex beneath their feet. "You sure about that?"

John had to grin. "Not anymore!"

Their pilot was running half crouched to meet a figure who had emerged from a stairwell. He clasped the man's hand, said something inaudible, then escorted him across the helipad toward them.

John squinted against the breeze. Their new host was tall, his black hair pulled back into a neat bun that somehow defied the violence of the wind that tugged at his loose shirt and pants. He didn't look like a teacher, thought John; he looked like he was on his way to some mountaintop retreat. He had incredibly bright eyes, so piercing that John almost flinched.

<31>

The man came to a stop in front of them and spread his arms wide as if he were encompassing the entire ocean.

"I am Yasuo Yamamoto," he smiled. "Welcome to the Wolf's Den!"

<<>>

That, John and Slack soon realized, was as friendly as Yasuo Yamamoto was ever going to get. By the time they were sitting cross-legged opposite him in a small zen garden, in a circular space filled with pale northern light, he had reverted to teacher mode: reserved, calm, and a lot more intimidating than Mrs. Long had ever been. He spent a long time simply staring into John's eyes, before turning his head and giving Slack the same penetrating gaze.

Slack was wriggling nervously. John wondered whether his friend needed to pee as much as he did.

After what felt like an eternity, Yasuo Yamamoto tilted back his head and stared up at the glass roof.

"Most of the time we leave it open," he remarked. "The sky brings light and clarity. Though it can also bring mysteries." He turned his gaze back to the boys.

"Uh," said Slack, "so you only do the vanishing-ground thing to impress newbies?"

Unexpectedly, the man laughed, all his solemnity gone like the snow sliding off the platform. "Yes, basically."

John felt a rush of relief. "Sorry, but are you the principal here, Mr. Yamamoto?"

"No." He shook his head. "And call me Yasuo, please. All teachers are addressed by their first names. Except Ms. Reiffelt, who *is*

<32>

the head teacher." He flashed another of those sudden grins. "I wouldn't go calling her Irma, if I were you."

"Thanks for the tip," said Slack, uncrossing his legs and stretching them.

"One of your fellow students will show you around," Yasuo said. "She'll be here shortly. In the meantime, you may ask me any questions. Though I can give you only the answers that I have."

He'd already treated them to four or five nuggets of obtuse wisdom. John wondered whether he was doing it deliberately.

"Well . . . we know you teach advanced computer science," John ventured. "But we don't know exactly what that means."

Yasuo closed his eyes. "This facility prides itself on recruiting the most technologically gifted students in the world," he intoned. "We shape and direct those skills to create the computing giants of tomorrow. Your abilities are raw; we hone them to skills that will one day benefit all. You are here because you have proved yourselves in ways that may have been—shall we say—morally dubious, or self-serving. Personal gain and mere entertainment will no longer be your motivation." His eyes snapped open, pinning them like bugs. "Here at the Wolf's Den Center, you will learn to penetrate and control the most secure systems in the world—and you will do it for the greater good."

John turned to Slack. Slack was staring at him with his mouth hanging open.

"Wow," said Slack. "I am *so in*."

"Indeed," drawled Yasuo with a slight smile, "you are."

John shook himself. "Anyway, that's the line from the brochure." He narrowed his eyes looking at Yasuo. "What do *you* teach?"

<33>

"Some things I teach," he said with a light shrug. "Mostly, like you, I learn."

John wanted to cry in frustration. "So who *does* teach?"

"Some names will be familiar to you." Yasuo uncurled himself and rose easily to his feet. "Howard McAuliffe. Imogen Black. Carlos Sanchez Ramirez. Roy Lykos—"

"Roy *Lykos*?" Slack's voice said with a high-pitched squeak. "Roy Lykos teaches here?"

John was rather glad he hadn't spoken; he was sure his voice would have been even more unsteady than Slack's. The names Yasuo had listed were a who's who of software innovators, but Roy Lykos was on a different level. A different *planet*, even.

"Lykos is a legend," he breathed at last. He reddened. "I mean, Mr. Lykos. I mean, Roy."

"Indeed he is." Yasuo turned to the gap in the polished sandstone wall that passed for a door. "Ah, Salome. Thank you for coming. These are our new arrivals, John Laine and Jake Hook. Please make them feel at home."

John scrambled to his feet. Polite manners weren't one of his instincts, but something about this girl demanded them.

Salome Abraham was very tall and slender, her skin as dark and smooth as polished ebony; she had almond-shaped eyes, high cheekbones, and an aloof tilt to her head. John had a feeling Slack's devotion to Akane was going to diminish as quickly as his crush on Leona.

Sure enough, Slack's voice beside him was little more than a croak: "Hi, Salome."

"Hello, Jake. Hello, John." Her gaze swept them up and down. "Come with me and I'll show you to your rooms."

<34>

"Call me Slack." He had recovered his composure and was flashing her his most charming smile.

"I might," said Salome, raising her eyebrows at Yasuo. John caught the teacher stifling a smile. "Now, if you've quite finished staring, can I show you the school?"

<<>>

"Are you left- or right-handed?" Salome halted and spun on her heels.

"Huh?" John glanced in confusion at Slack. "Right, um . . . "

"Then give me your right hand."

Suspiciously, John did as he was told. Salome took it firmly and drew a slender glass device from her pocket. In one swift movement, she pressed it down into John's palm.

"What the—"

She looked at him quizzically. "It didn't hurt, did it?"

John stared at his palm. The puncture mark was tiny and had reddened only a little. He hadn't felt a thing.

Salome had already turned to Slack. "Now you."

"Left," said Slack, almost defiantly, and had thrust out his hand before John could form the words, "Don't, Slack, don't cooperate; this seems a bit invasive."

"It's your nano implant," Salome told them casually. "Opens all kinds of doors."

Slack was staring at a tiny red mark on his palm that was already fading. Glancing up, he met John's eyes. *Weird*, he mouthed.

Creepy, John mouthed back, clenching his fist.

<35>

Salome didn't even mention the implant again. Her shoes clicked sharply as she strode ahead down an opaque glass and chrome-railed walkway that glowed pale blue with hidden lights. It felt to John as if he were walking on a bed of clouds. "You'll be tested, of course," she told them. "The results will determine whose classes you can attend. What did you do to get here, anyway?"

The two boys exchanged a guilty look. "This and that," said Slack at last. "Hacking phones and credit card numbers, for me. One time, John broke the US Department of Defense's firewall."

"Yeah, that and my sister's Snapchat," John grinned. "What about you, Salome? What did you get up to?"

The look she threw him could have frozen a lava flow. "I didn't *get up to* anything," she said acerbically. "Unless you count winning a computer science scholarship to Princeton."

"Oh" was all John could say.

"At your age?" Slack's eyes boggled.

"I didn't take it," she told them with a toss of her braided hair. "My father said this place would be more challenging. The sheer intensity of the work means I can graduate sooner and start making a positive contribution to the world. And it will open up better opportunities."

"Oh," said John again, hoarsely. *Positive contribution to the world?* This girl was terrifying.

"This is Roy Lykos's classroom." Salome stopped to place her palm against a glowing sensor, and the glass door slid silently open. "You'll only work with him if your test results are the best."

"Let me guess," muttered Slack. "You're in his class."

"Of course I am." She stepped inside.

<36>

"I think I'll stick with Akane," Slack whispered to John as he followed her.

John started to grin, but it faded as he stepped inside. "Wow," he said.

It was more like an auditorium than a classroom, with a sweeping semicircle of tiered seats that faced a lectern and a massive screen. Each seat had a curved acrylic desk on its right, but only a few of them were equipped with translucent flat-screen monitors—*nine*, John realized, counting them in his head. So this vast room, he guessed, was used by only a small, elite group of students.

Ten monitors by next week, he promised himself silently. *No, eleven. Slack will get into Lykos's class too.*

After all, not only was Slack as smart as he was—but also John didn't think he could bear lessons with only the humorless, morally uptight Salome for company.

Salome was already ushering them out of the sacred class-room. "And that room over there is where you'll take your tests. It's really basic; you don't need to see it. I'll show you your dorm now. Oh. Hello, Eva."

There was something in Salome's voice that made John curi-ous. He turned as the girl named Eva strode past, glanced twice at them, then stopped.

John thought maybe she was about the same age as them, but it was hard to tell. She was very small and slight. Her spiky blond hair, pulled back in a rough ponytail, was so pale it was almost as white as her delicate face—which looked as if she'd never seen the sun. Even so, she'd outlined her eyes heavily with black. It shouldn't have worked with her complexion, but it

<37>

matched her leather jacket, her ripped black jeans, and her heavy boots. Eva may have been a head shorter than both John and Slack, but she was instantly intimidating.

"Yeah. Hi, Salome." Eva had a slight tinge of an accent—Russian, maybe?—but what her voice mainly conveyed was boredom. "New boys?"

Salome nodded eagerly. "Just arrived. This is John, and that's Jake."

"Slack," added Slack.

Salome ignored him. "Are you going to Hack Club later, Eva?"

The pale girl shrugged. "Maybe. If I'm not busy."

"Hope to see you there, then!" Salome raised a hand to say goodbye, but Eva didn't return her wave. She just marched off down the walkway and turned into a classroom. The door slid silently closed.

"She seems friendly," John observed. "Not."

Salome sighed, but it sounded more wistful than impatient this time. "She's interesting. Really, really smart, but I think she's shy."

The girl hadn't seemed shy at all to John, but he decided not to press. "What's her accent? Where's she from?"

Salome gave a shrug. "The funny thing is nobody knows. The first records of her are from when she was found in a compartment on the Trans-Siberian Express. That was in Ulaanbaatar, but nobody knows where she got on—not even Eva. She didn't have a clue who she was, where she was from, or how she'd gotten on the train. All she knew was her name."

"Wow," said Slack, staring at the spot where Eva had disappeared. "Mystery girl."

<38>

"She must have had papers," said John, frowning. "Like, a passport?"

"No passport, no suitcase, no documents." There was longing curiosity in Salome's expression. "Nobody ever claimed her, either. I guess that's why she's so prickly. But I don't know *why* nobody did. She's super bright. Speaks German, French, and Italian. And Russian, of course, though I don't know why I say 'of course,' because nobody even knows whether she's really Russian. And she plays piano and violin like a pro. And that's before you get to her computing skills, which are *amazing*."

It was the most Salome had said to them since they'd left Yasuo's garden "office," and John blinked in surprise and raised his eyebrows at Slack.

"So, like I said—she's interesting." Salome shrugged again and turned to lead them onward.

John found himself warming to Salome for the first time; it seemed the statuesque beauty was human after all. It was painfully obvious that she wanted to be friends with Eva—and that Eva couldn't be less interested. *Poor Salome. I bet she isn't used to being rejected.*

"How about you?" he asked. "Where are you from?"

"Ethiopia," she told him, "though I'm from all over, really. My dad's a diplomat. OK, here's your room."

John stared at the blank door. No handle, no lock, no touch-sensor. "And, er . . . how do we get into it?"

"Dormitories are of course more private than the other rooms. Look at me."

<39>

He'd obeyed automatically before he could think about it. The light she flashed into his right eye blinded him only briefly, but it was long enough for Salome to do the same to Slack.

"OK. Now look at the door."

Hesitantly, John turned, blinking. A light glowed around the edges of the door, and it slid open.

"Oh," said Slack, raising his eyebrows. "Cool."

"Iris recognition? Could this *get* any more intrusive?" John felt his annoyance rising. "What does the school do with that data? I mean, it's like—"

"You get to settle in tonight," Salome interrupted him, ignoring his outburst. "And your tests are at eight tomorrow morning."

"Eight?" Slack almost shrieked, as John pursed his lips sulkily. "No time to study?"

Salome made a face. "No point in studying. They're testing your skills. You pass, or you don't."

"OK," said John, taking a deep breath. What was the point in protesting? He hadn't consented to the nano implants or the iris recognition, but they were done deals, and presumably it wasn't Salome's decision. If it happened to everybody, they'd just have to accept it. Besides, he was almost scared to ask, but his belly was rumbling embarrassingly loudly, and Salome was pretending not to notice: "When's dinner?"

"When you want it. You can get pastries and smoothies at that place we passed. Go down the corridor I showed you and there's a sushi bar. Also salad, burgers, Thai food, Korean, tapas, Japanese barbecue, and vegetarian—"

"Seriously?" There was a look of ravenous greed on Slack's face.

<40>

"Seriously. Whenever you're hungry, as long as you aren't in class. Don't be late tomorrow morning!" For the very first time, Salome smiled properly at them. "And good luck."

As she marched off back the way they'd come, John stared at the inner surface of the door, and it slid gently closed once more. Turning, the two boys gazed around their new room.

It was minimalist but not exactly basic: two beds, two desks, two separate, stylish sinks, and big cupboards that fit flush with the paneled walls. A huge glass screen took up most of another wall; it was set so smoothly into the paneling that at first John mistook it for a window. Two gaming keyboards and two game controllers were set neatly beneath it, and Slack snatched one up.

The glass leaped to life, and a monstrous alien soldier turned and took a step into the room. Slack stumbled back and fell over.

The heavily armored infantryman turned right and left, fingering his weapon. He looked as if he were waiting for his orders.

"It's 3-D," whispered Slack, scrambling to his feet. "And you don't need glasses."

It looked so solid, so real, that when John stepped forward, merging himself with the avatar, he let out a gasp of surprise. Backing off, he flopped down on one of the beds and felt the crispest sheets and the softest quilt he'd ever been lucky enough to touch.

"How d'you think they got all this stuff to the island?" he murmured. "Must have been a heck of a logistics problem. Did you see the port as we flew over?"

"No . . . " said Slack, frowning. He touched a light on his game controller, and the soldier vanished.

<41>

"Exactly. There isn't one. They must have flown all the construction materials in. And the fittings. And the electronics. And the workers to build it. In this climate. I mean, *wow*."

"Somebody," said Slack solemnly, "has hacked a *lot* of credit card details. Well, that, or somebody is fabulously rich."

"I wish we could contact the outside world, though. That's a bummer."

"Wish we could *what*?"

John threw a pillow at him. "I knew you weren't listening to Salome. No email, no messaging, certainly no FaceTime. Our phones will be regularly spot-checked to make sure they're offline, and if there's a live connection? Expulsion. We get ten minutes a week with our families on the landline."

"But—" Slack's face fell. "That means you don't get to talk to Akane."

"I just knew that'd be the first thing in your head." John sighed and slumped back. "But yeah. That's going to be horrible."

"Why that rule?" Slack said sulkily. "Doesn't make sense."

"Something to do with security. Anyway, I guess it's a small price to pay." John pulled a book on Inuit mythology out of his bag. "I'll catch up on my reading."

Slack looked pointedly at the screen. "Or we could play the heck out of the latest *Call of Duty* . . ."

John set the book down and grinned. "I think I'm going to like this school . . ."

<42>

Five

"How did you do?" John muttered to Slack as their
screens went simultaneously blank then lit up with a sleek logo:
Wolf's Den Center.

"Oh man," Slack whispered back. "I looked at that coding
problem, and I just had *no clue.*"

"Didn't look that way to me," said John, surprised. "You were
typing like a crazy person."

"You too," Slack pointed out.

"Yeah, but that was because—I don't know—because I suddenly felt a weird—" John frowned, then whispered as he glanced
toward the front. "Sh!"

Everyone in the test class had fallen silent, including the su-
pervising teacher. The glass doors parted as if opened by invisible
footmen, and a tall figure strode into the room. He turned on his
heels, clasped his hands behind his back, and gazed at the class.
His face was instantly recognizable from a thousand technology
news stories and computing magazines, let alone *Time*'s Man of
the Year issue. If Zeus had strode down from Mount Olympus,
John's jaw could not have dropped further.

"It's him," squeaked Slack, faintly.

John said nothing, only swallowed. Roy Lykos's piercing blue eyes had fixed briefly on Slack as he spoke. They shifted to John then continued to roam around among the other test candidates.

"Good morning, ladies and gentlemen."

The voice was rich and mellifluous, with a hint of good humor. It was a little at odds with Lykos's austere looks: the close-cropped, almost colorless hair; the black turtleneck; the beautifully cut black pants. John glanced self-consciously down at his own flea-market jeans and discovered that for the first time in his life he wanted something a little more designer.

He looked back up at Lykos. Those pale eyes were locked on him and Slack. Suddenly, Roy Lykos smiled, and it was as if the Alaskan sun had come out.

"The good news is your test results won't take long to come through," he said. "We'll assign your classes later today. Until then, I suggest you all relax and get to know the Center a little better. When your work starts, it'll be intense. I won't say the most important thing is to enjoy your time here—that's definitely *not* the most important thing!—but take advantage of the facilities when you can." Yet again, his gaze slid back to John and Slack. "Everybody needs time to reboot!"

A ripple of slightly anxious laughter went around the classroom, and the new students began to rise. There were no bags to gather up; none had been allowed into the room. As John and Slack joined the line of students at the door, John felt a tingling on his neck, and he turned. Lykos was still watching him and Slack as he murmured to another teacher. Feeling a little starstruck, John risked a smile.

<44>

Excusing himself from his conversation, Roy Lykos strode over to them as the class emptied. "Welcome to the Wolf's Den, you two."

Slack gazed up at him in awe. "Hi . . . uh, hi, Mr. Lykos."

"It's Roy." He grinned. "You're John and Jake, right? You've both done well. I monitor the tests as they're happening."

A surge of delight went through John, making him blush. He'd always known he was good, but he'd had more than a twinge of uncertainty as he entered the classroom: some of the kids here had looked terrifyingly composed and clever. And that moment of understanding as he stared at the coding problem had felt more like a lucky lightning strike than a rational problem-solving decision.

But Roy Lykos has singled us out! His chest swelled with pride.

"By the way, I didn't tell you how you did, OK?" Roy winked. "But you'll all be getting your results and class assignments in a couple of hours, so I don't see the harm in it. I think it's safe to say you'll both be joining my classes."

"Yes!" Losing his composure, Slack punched the air.

Roy laughed. "Go on—take out the stress in the gym. The hard work starts tomorrow."

As he raised a hand in farewell and strode off through the classroom doors, John and Slack turned to give each other broad grins and a high five.

"We did it!" said John.

"I honestly thought we were doomed when I saw that coding puzzle." Slack wiped his forehead dramatically. "But I had a flash of inspiration while I stared at it."

"Same!" John grinned, shrugging. "Isn't that weird? It just made sense . . . all of a sudden. Like it just clicked in my brain."

<45>

"It was all about the traversal approach, right?"

"Yes! Hey, we must be psychic!"

"Not psychic," said Slack grandly. "Just geniuses. Want to celebrate with a burger?"

"You ever stop thinking about food?" John punched his arm.

They slapped and shoved each other playfully, competing to be first through the door, so it took John a moment to notice that the crowd in the outside corridor had fallen silent. Only when Slack froze, his eyes popping out of his head, did John turn and follow his gaze.

The other test candidates stood respectfully as a woman strode down the glowing walkway. She wasn't particularly tall, but no wonder everyone had stopped talking: she moved with the arrogance of someone who could have them all executed on the spot. Her cropped hair was the same iron gray as her suit, her face was sharp boned, and her eyes were practically black behind jet-rimmed cat-eye glasses. She was not smiling. But maybe, thought John, that didn't mean much. She didn't look like she *ever* smiled. Staring at her, John felt a tremor of steely cold run down his spine.

The woman's heels clicked to a halt beside Roy Lykos, and she pivoted to face him with almost military precision.

"Roy, my boy," she said into the silence. "How did your tests go this morning?"

Roy smiled easily at her. "Hello, Irma. Very well, as a matter of fact. Very well, indeed." He glanced around, and his eyes met John's. They were twinkling.

"Good morning, candidates." The woman turned from Roy, and her gaze swept around among the gathered students. The corners

<46>

of her lips didn't even twitch. "I am Ms. Reiffelt, the principal. Welcome to the Wolf's Den Center."

"Good morning, Ms. Reiffelt." Even Slack joined in the automatic and slightly terrified chorus.

"It is a pleasure to welcome talented students," she said, though it didn't sound as if it was much of a pleasure. Her accent had a touch of Eastern Europe, John thought, and her tone could have sliced through the glass roof. "You are all here because you have remarkable skills, but it will be to your benefit if you assume, in this school, that you are not as able as you believe. Keep in mind that, until your learning proceeds, in this place you are all—how do you put it?—script kiddies."

Beside him, John felt Slack bristle. His friend's blue eyes were glowering with resentment. *That's more like it,* thought John with a secret grin. And Slack's defiance made him feel a bit less intimidated himself.

"I look forward to watching your skills develop." Irma Reiffelt gave a brisk nod, and there was a tiny tightening of her lips that might have been the start of a formal smile. Before it could turn into one, she had walked away.

John shook himself as the other students began to talk once again, this time in low murmurs. "Phew," he said.

"What a monster," growled Slack. "I take back every mean thing I ever said about Mrs. Long. She's a cuddly sweetheart next to that—that—"

"Gorgon," suggested John. "She could turn you to stone with one look."

"Don't mind Ms. Reiffelt." Roy walked back to their side, his eyes warm with amusement. "She's scary, but she's an excellent teacher

<47>

who gets results. And I'm looking forward to seeing you both in class tomorrow. Script kiddies you are not."

Slack grinned. "Yeah, we know."

"Buuut . . . she's right. You will learn things here you never imagined were possible." Roy winked. "I know from your tests that you turn left where everyone else would turn right. That's to be expected from any competent hacker. Here you'll learn to turn upward instead and cross to another dimension."

"Yeah!" Slack's eyes glittered with excitement.

"We can't wait," said John, his heart racing.

Roy grinned. "Welcome to Hackwarts."

John laughed and raised a nervous hand in farewell as Roy turned away. He felt Slack tug his sleeve.

"What's wrong with *them*?" hissed his friend, jerking his thumb.

John followed his gesture. Across the vast, sunny atrium, two boys were glaring at them. One was tall and muscular looking— quite the jock, if it hadn't been for his austere black T-shirt and pants and his hipster glasses. The other was shorter, with curly, dark hair and angry, flashing eyes. His style wasn't much like his friend's; he wore a preppy blue polo shirt and chinos.

"Looks like he got lost on the way to the golf course," snorted Slack.

Frowning, John returned the boys' stares. "What's making them so mad? Big ninja guy looks like he wants to throttle us with a Calvin Klein sports towel."

Slack shrugged as the boys threw them one last glare before marching away.

"Dunno. But I have a feeling we're going to find out . . . "

<48>

Six

"Do not imagine," said Ms. Reiffelt, **"that I have** illusions about some of you here today. There are students in this class who are here through hard study and dedication. And there are some students here because they are *criminals*."

Her eyes were the color of icy slate, and they were fixed on John and Slack. John swallowed as a blade of sharp guilt slid under his sternum, but Slack didn't even flinch. He was slouching at his desk next to John, a slight smile tugging at the corner of his mouth.

To John, there was no disguising the light of eagerness in his friend's eyes, but he didn't think that would be enough to placate their steely principal.

Ms. Reiffelt's eyes lingered on Slack a little longer, then she gave an almost imperceptible nod. "Hacking is no laughing matter—"

"Looks like nothing is," muttered Slack under his breath.

"—but it can be a very worthwhile endeavor. At this Center, ladies and gentlemen, you will learn to combat those who do as you once did. Far from committing crimes, you will find them and undo them. You will learn to protect individuals and systems

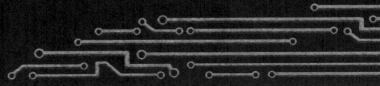

against those who would do them harm." She paused. "Unless, of course, we *want* you to do them harm."

Slack sat up a little straighter, balancing his unused pencil deftly between his fingers.

"You all know that worms can be used to destroy defense systems, for instance. There may be some systems that are—shall we say—asking for it."

Slack's expression was positively enthusiastic now, and clearly he could contain himself no longer. "What's your specialty, Ms. Reiffelt?"

She turned back to him. Irma Reiffelt was very good at long, heavy silences, thought John.

"Cryptanalysis," she said at last, coolly. "I will teach you to break impossible codes and also to write them. Both of which, incidentally, I have spent much of my life doing at a practical level. I believe you consider yourself quite special, Mr. Hook, and you appear to resent the term 'script kiddie.'" A knowing and slightly unpleasant smile twitched at the corner of her mouth. "While I dislike it myself, I can assure you that compared to me, it suits you well."

There were snickers behind them, and John turned his head. The boy he'd noticed in the atrium, the one with the black T-shirt and hipster glasses, was openly smirking at Slack, and his curly haired friend could barely suppress his laughter.

The rest of the class was silent, studiously avoiding Slack's reddening face, but down at the front Eva Vygotsky turned, propping her elbow on her desk so that she could stare at him.

"Ms. Reiffelt worked for many years for the intelligence services of the DDR," she said.

<50>

John expected Ms. Reiffelt to snap at the Russian girl, but she only nodded, giving Eva an approving smile.

Wait, he thought, *the DDR? East Germany?*

"Servers are protected against data theft," the teacher went on, as if Eva hadn't spoken, "but as you are all aware, hackers can always break through. It's your job, among other things, to make that more difficult for them. Today we will begin building a practical system that will compute encrypted data without access to the decryption key. And when I say 'practical,' I mean exactly that. I shall expect you to come up with a combination of systems and cryptography that will be *fast,* rather than cripplingly slow."

Her face, thought John, held more than expectation: she looked as if she'd have them all shot if they didn't come up to par.

"During this term we shall build a database system, a web application platform, and a mobile system. Kindly take written notes as we begin. In some ways, I am old-fashioned." Suddenly, her eyes swept up the rows of desks and landed on the boys behind John and Slack. "Adam Kruz! Leonidas Pallikaris! This also applies to you. I specify this because you so often believe that my instructions do *not.*"

John glanced back with a grin. The boys looked really uncomfortable; they were shifting in their seats, and a fierce flush crept up the curly haired one's cheekbones.

She doesn't have favorites, he realized with relief. *She'll have a go at anybody. Even—what did she call them?—Adam and Leonidas.* He filed the names in his head, certain he was going to run into those two boys again.

"Miss Vygotsky is correct about my career," Ms. Reiffelt told them all, as her own keyboard lit up and glinted on her cat-eye glasses. "Needless to say I will be providing no juicy details,

<51>

but what I will say is this: hacking is espionage for a new generation. I served my former state, and I served this one. And should your country need you—even when your country itself believes that it does not—you *will* be there for it."

John swallowed hard.

"Now," Ms. Reiffelt said, "let us begin."

<<>>

"Phew," muttered Slack as they closed their laptops. "My head hurts."

"Script kiddie," John laughed.

"Go on, admit it. You've got the start of the biggest migraine in the world."

"Not just the start of it," admitted John. "But c'mon, that was fun."

Slack grinned. "I think by the end of this week I'm going to be sick of the sight of computers."

"Never happen," said John.

As the class set off past the rows of desks toward the door, Eva Vygotsky paused to talk to Ms. Reiffelt, who leaned close and listened intently. *If she* does *have a favorite,* thought John as he watched them, *it's definitely Eva.*

"We'd better get going. We're due in"—Slack checked his phone—"Yasuo's classroom. Five minutes. Denial of Service tutorial. Hey, I've done that!"

"Yeah, when you shut off the heating system in the school in Fairbanks. I've got a feeling this is going to be a bit more challenging."

"Got us all a day off, didn't I?" Slack smirked. "Yeah, but from the way things are going, I'm guessing we'll be stopping World War Three. Or starting it, maybe."

"Look at these classes and it's only week one." John took out his own phone and scrolled down the calendar. "Bot Armies: The Art of War. The Walking Dead: Zombie Traffic and the Collapse of Web Services. Looking a Trojan Horse in the Mouth: who came up with *that* dumb title?"

"I did."

John didn't even have to look up. He decided the best strategy was to go on staring at his phone screen till the flood of embarrassment subsided.

When he did, Roy Lykos was watching him with sharp amusement.

John cleared his throat. "Sorry, Mr.—I mean, Roy."

"Never apologize, John." Roy laughed. "I thought twice about that title myself, but I wanted something catchy for Mr. McAuliffe's—for Howard's—course." He leaned a little closer and whispered, "Because, to be honest, it's a little dull."

John couldn't help spluttering a laugh. "OK."

"Mr. Lykos. Are you distracting students, my boy?" Ms. Reiffelt strode out of the classroom behind them. "Because I'm sure they have somewhere to be."

John saw a flash of irritation on Roy's face at her patronizing "my boy," but he took a step back. That, though, wasn't as surprising as the look he gave Eva Vygotsky.

The Russian girl was walking out of the classroom, her laptop clutched against her chest. As she caught sight of Roy, she neither hurried up nor slowed her pace, but she caught his eye and held it. Eva's expression was unreadable, but Roy's darkened.

Fascinated, John watched the silent, hostile interaction. Was that anger in the man's eyes? It looked an awful lot like it. But there was something else there too, and he could swear it was fear.

<53>

He had to be imagining that. As Eva strode off down the corridor, John gave himself an inward shake. "We're scheduled for one of your classes this afternoon, Roy." It still felt odd to call a teacher by his first name. "We're looking forward to it."

Lykos's eyes seemed to focus again. "And so you should be," he said, his relaxed charm restored. "We'll be starting to investigate advanced infrastructure hacking. Intercepting HTTPS connections and forcing them to use weakened encryption. You like the sound of that?"

"Yeah." Slack's eyes shone. "*Freakin'* awesome!"

Ms. Reiffelt shot him a look of cold disapproval. "You two should be in Yasuo's classroom by now. Please get going. Roy, my boy, we have a meeting at four, don't we?"

It didn't seem like a real question, and her eyes were challenging. Roy simply nodded, but his voice was cool. "I'll see you in Lab 31, Irma. Till later, you two."

As John and Slack hurried away, John glanced back over his shoulder and caught Roy's wink. He grinned to himself.

"What was that all about?" he asked Slack.

"I dunno, John, but that woman is terrifying. Roy doesn't like her."

"Yeah, I noticed. Heck, she was a communist spy, though! Being scary is probably in the job description."

"I don't know about you," said Slack with feeling, "but I've got a real hankering now for a few Zen-like nuggets of obscure wisdom. And we're late for Yasuo."

"Makes me hanker for a sloppy joe," grinned John. "Come on, we'd better run!"

<54>

Seven

There was something very reassuring about the climbing wall, thought John, but for a few moments after he stepped in front of it, he couldn't figure out what it was. Then he realized: *It's solid and ordinary. It's a big textured fiberglass wall with handholds. It's not going to give me a screen headache.*

He grinned, clipping his harness with a carabiner. Physical effort wasn't his favorite thing—he'd been the worst hockey player in either Vancouver or Fairbanks and the last pick for everybody's baseball team—but he was amazed at how enticing it was now.

Any excuse to disengage my brain for ten minutes.

It was an odd sensation but not unpleasant. His mind felt like a blank screen but not a faulty one: he could just let it relax into sleep mode for a while. *Information will download in the background. The programs are initiated; let them run.*

What was wrong with him? It must be all that coding home-work; he was starting to *think* like a laptop. Grinning, he reached out and seized a molded grip.

He was *not* expecting the wallpaper.

The artificial surface was gone. He was standing at the foot of a vast sandstone butte, its flanks gilded by the Arizona sun, and there was warm, dusty rock beneath his fingertips. With a yelp of surprise, he startled backward, and the wall was once again a fiberglass construction in a small, glass-walled room. Furrowing his brow, half-smiling, John reached out once more for the resin grip—and in an instant, he was back in Monument Valley.

"Wow," he muttered, impressed. *So much for switching off from the digital world.*

"One of my favorite new products," said an amused voice. "But a bit expensive to take to market just yet."

Poised on the lowest grips, John twisted to see Roy Lykos approaching across the red desert sand. *No*, he thought, *he's walking through a perfectly ordinary room.* "It's pretty impressive!"

Roy glanced up and around as he pulled on his climbing shoes. "If the sun's too much, there's a rock face in the Andes," he mused. "Or the Old Man of Hoy in Orkney—it's thoroughly overcast there."

"This is just fine." John grinned.

"Good." Roy nodded with approval. "I like Arizona. Plenty of space to think." He gripped a small outcrop of rock, then gave John a wink. "The nano implants are good for more than recalling your food preferences."

They certainly were, and suddenly John didn't mind the intrusiveness of them. "I always wanted to learn to climb." He hesitated, a little embarrassed. "My dad was really good at it."

"I'm amazed he had time."

John glanced at Roy, startled. "You know about him?"

<56>

"You could say that." Roy paused his climb. "I did presentations at medical conferences. He was a fine man, with much to contribute to the world. I'm so sorry about what happened."

"Me too." The words caught in John's throat.

"He'd be proud of you, John. That's quite a talent you have." Roy reached for another grabhold and pulled himself higher.

"Thank you." John felt his cheeks burning as red as the digital rock face.

"I mean it. Your computing abilities are almost a natural instinct. They fascinate me."

John twisted to look at the desert floor, far below. It wasn't frightening. The illusion was convincing and made the ascent seem higher than it could possibly be, but his brain knew it was just that: an illusion. He paused to catch his breath and to compose himself, hanging by one hand. "My dad would have liked me to go into medicine," he mumbled at last.

For a moment, Roy didn't speak. He seemed entirely focused on hauling himself up the overhang above him. When he finally rested, he looked down at John, and there was understanding and kindness in his face.

"Maybe, John, but do you think he'd be disappointed if you didn't? He wouldn't. Your father was a great man, and he was respected for a reason. He was the best at what he did. I think *that* is what he'd want for you. And one day, John, you will be the best at what *you* do. At what you *love*."

John had been fumbling for a foothold; as his shoe caught it, he felt a surge of pride mixed with embarrassment. *Did Roy Lykos really just say that?* Almost without thinking, he reached for the last grips and hauled himself up to the overhang. He sat

<57>

down panting beside Roy, and they stared together over the wild desertscape.

"I hope you're right," he muttered, pushing back his hair. "Thanks."

"No need to thank me." Roy rested a hand on his shoulder and turned to him, his face serious. "I *know* I'm right, John. There's something in you that's special, and it's going to take you right to the top. Trust me."

John swallowed hard. "I do."

"Good." Roy was brisk again. "Speaking of the top, I think we're finished here. The next stretch isn't for beginners, and I think, in this one thing . . ."

"I'm a complete amateur." John laughed. He was amazed he'd gotten this far up the butte—maybe following Roy's lead had been the secret. "My dad gave me a few lessons, but he didn't really have much time . . ." He didn't want to dwell on that. "Anyway, yeah, I'd better go. I've got a class with Imogen Black in twenty minutes."

"Better get going, then." Roy smiled. "I know the work here seems unremitting, but in your case in particular, it's going to be totally worth it. By the way, if you want your climbing to improve, Yasuo's your man. And he always has time for students. Just go to his room and ask—his door's always open. Literally."

"OK. I will!" John grinned.

"Now," said Roy, his eyes suddenly intent. "Climbing up is the easy part. Let's see you rappel . . ."

<58>

Eight

Akane gave a strangled yell of frustration and shoved her chair back from her desk.

"Akane?" Obaasan's voice drifted through from the next room. "Is something wrong?"

"Nothing, Grandmother!" called Akane hastily. "Stubbed my toe."

The old woman seemed to accept that; Akane could hear her gossiping once again with Mrs. Hagashi from next door. Relieved, she turned back to her computer screen.

No wonder John hadn't been in touch, she thought, reading again in mounting irritation. *What a stupid rule. I thought it was a school for computer geeks?*

Landline, indeed. And a ten-minute call once a week! Only to immediate family!

Rules, she thought as she clenched her jaw, were there to be broken. Especially for people like her and John. She interlinked her fingers and flexed them then set to typing furiously.

Of course, she should have anticipated that the Wolf's Den security would be troublesome. Every way she turned, there seemed to be firewalls and barriers and tricky little misdirections. They did *not* want their students having outside contact, she realized, as yet another ACCESS DENIED message flashed at her.

I'm Akane Maezono, she reminded herself. *I'm a White Eye Hoax Hunter. And if they want me to turn right, I'll turn left.*

She exited the tempting little window that popped up. Closing one eye, biting her lip, she clicked back to coding mode and typed again. Someone at the Wolf's Den thought they could beat her, did they? Whoever it was, they were making her angry now. And when Akane got angry, she didn't lose her temper. No way. If anything, she got cooler than ever: cool enough to see things out of the corner of her eye, like floaters in her peripheral vision. And *those* were usually the things they least wanted her to see.

Akane sat back, tapping her fingernails against the edge of the desk. If someone was this keen to stop outside contact, they were bound to have spent less time protecting other files.

Like the staff dossiers, maybe . . . Akane grinned.

Oh, she *loved* it when this happened. As if there was a second screen inside her head, she knew suddenly and completely what she had to do. The code came to her so smoothly and swiftly she could barely type fast enough to keep up.

She wasn't even sure she *was* keeping up. As her fingers flew across the keyboard, lines of encrypted code rippled into a blur across her vision. There was something transcendent about this feeling. She'd heard of it happening to other people, in other ways: artists, maybe, when the pencil or the paintbrush took over, or soldiers, when they slipped into an automatic, fluid combat mode. Excitement made her scalp tingle, but she kept typing:

<60>

it was like a duel, but in a strange way, the program wasn't just fighting her; it was *dancing* with her. She could almost hear the beat and pulse of the music . . .

Akane gave a high, hoarse gasp as she snapped her hands back from the keys. ACCESS GRANTED.

"Akane? Is everything all right?" Sharp knuckles rapped on the door.

For a moment Akane was so out of breath she couldn't answer.

"Akane?"

"It's fine, Obaasan!" She licked her lips and cleared her throat. "It's fine, uh . . . I thought my computer crashed, but it's OK. Don't worry!"

"Well, don't worry me so! I've been knocking for a long time. Food is almost ready."

As she listened to her grandmother's footsteps shuffling away, Akane closed her eyes and heaved a sigh of relief. Then she opened them again and stared at the screen.

That name. What's that name doing there?

She'd told Obaasan everything was fine. But it wasn't. It wasn't fine at all.

John must know. Surely John knew?

No, thought Akane. If John had known, he would have told her. And John said he'd never even heard of the Center before he was ordered to go there.

The bigger question was *Should* John be told? It was an odd enough coincidence that Mikael Laine had been a director of the Wolf's Den Center—and what on earth did a neurosurgeon have

<61>

to do with computer technology anyway?—but it was even odder that his name hadn't yet been removed from the list of directors.

OK, he was only *presumed* dead, but still. It would be so upsetting for John to see his father's name there, as if nothing had happened, as if he were still alive. It might even give him false hope. Not to mention the shock of realizing his father had a prior connection with his new school.

There was a familiar buzzing at the back of her brain, one that had been there for a year. Akane thought of it as a background program that she kept running, working out an old and bewildering enigma while she focused on current day-to-day problems. She never discovered how John had, out of nowhere, downloaded a key to her own private system to act as her unwanted virtual ground crew. The intrigue had long ago overtaken her annoyance at her BASE jump being thwarted.

Especially since, she could truly admit now, John had been *right*.

It was odd, though, that she felt that background program running now. Somewhere in her mind, she must have found a connection between this mystery and that infuriating, long-standing one. Human brains, she mused wryly, could be even more puzzling than computers.

Akane narrowed her eyes and cracked her fingers. She'd already found the weak spot in the Wolf's Den. And where there was one weak spot, there were only slightly stronger spots that relied on the exact same security measures. She'd always had a good instinct for where to start exploring, and the tickle in her brain told her that now that she'd found the list of directors, their email addresses were not going to be many connections away.

It was time to go phishing.

<62>

Nine

Those angry eyes. They were a threat. The boy should be neutralized.

John didn't know how he was a danger, but all that mattered was that the boy was wrong. The pastel preppy clothes were wrong. The dark curly hair was wrong. Everything about him had to go. For John's safety. For Slack's. For everyone's.

The boy did not even resist when John leaned close to him and wrapped his hands around his throat. His eyes still flashed with fury, but he didn't fight at all. And it took nothing. Barely a squeeze of John's fingers. Like a hologram, the boy flickered, and buzzed, and dissipated to nothing. The last thing left of him was those angry eyes, blazing into John's. And then those, too, faded out like a lightbulb.

John didn't care that he'd killed the boy. Why should he care? All that mattered was that John was safe now.

Except that there was that other boy, the one with the muscles and the black T-shirt. There he stood, right in front of John, and he had to be eliminated too—

John was startled awake, breathing hard. Across the room, Slack was snoring violently, but John was grateful: his friend's snorting grunts must have woken him.

Reaching for his water bottle, John wiped his hand across his face and felt cold sweat. That dream had been horrible. It hadn't been bloody or gory, but that murder had felt *real*. He'd killed Leo Pallikaris, and he hadn't cared. Worse, he'd been *glad* he did. A thrilling sense of a job well done clung to him.

And a nagging feeling that the task was not complete yet, that Adam Kruz was still alive . . .

He threw off the quilt and got up, his legs shaking slightly. Reaching for his phone, he checked the time.

"Slack!" he yelled. He shook his friend. "It's half past eleven!"

"Mumph," grunted Slack. "It's Saturday. Five more minutes . . . "

"You want to eat?" demanded John. "Because Hack Club starts in thirty minutes . . . "

"Wait, breakfast?" Instantly alert, Slack jumped out of bed. "You should have said so in the first place . . . "

<<>>

It was no wonder they'd slept in, thought John as he watched Slack cram another pastry into his mouth. The past few weeks had been exhaustingly intense, and being in Roy Lykos's classes had turned out to be a very mixed blessing. John still felt prouder than he'd been about anything in his life—but his brain was fried. In this past week alone they'd hacked a Russian missile system, gained access to the next Marvel movie plot, and brought down the entire British broadband network.

<64>

It might be wrong of him, but he wished it hadn't all been a simulation. The excitement had felt very real, but every hack they devised, every security wall they breached, was part of a gigantic offline virtual world: Global Two.

"It's just as well I've turned over a new leaf," said Slack, through a mouthful of Danish. "What I could do to Madison Harper now . . . "

"Use her phone to fire a nuclear warhead at Fairbanks Junior High," suggested John with a grin. "Two birds with one—ow!"

"Don't even think about it," scolded the passing Salome, as John winced and rubbed the back of his head. "Don't *talk* about it, for sure. You want to be expelled?" She sat down with her tray and glowered at both of them.

"No, Salome," said John sheepishly.

"Well, don't even joke. And don't boast. The teachers don't like it."

"Yeah, yeah. Because we're *script kiddies*," said Slack.

"You are. Certainly next to Roy," she said primly. "You'd better get a move on, by the way. Leo and Adam always get to Hack Club early, and if you want to beat them—"

"What is it with those two?" complained Slack. "They took an instant dislike to us."

Salome shrugged. "You got into Roy's class, which was bad enough. But you're getting a lot of his attention too. They've been his favorites till now." She sighed. "But don't worry. And don't get too comfortable either. Roy's favorites change by the day."

"How about you?" asked Slack. "You coming to Hack Club?"

"Of course." Salome relaxed, sipping on an espresso. "But I set up my hack last night. All I have to do is press a button. I'll see you in ten minutes."

<65>

"Wow," whispered Slack as the two boys walked away. "She's terrifying."

"Salome might be, but Adam and Leo aren't. We can take them, no problem." John gestured across the atrium. "Look, there they are. Salome was right—they're getting a jump on everybody else."

Adam and Leo were jogging down the stairway at the far end of the atrium, toward the basement—the one place in the complex that sunlight didn't reach. The location made Hack Club feel like even more of a guilty secret, but it gave it an extra edge of excitement too. After all, the club wasn't meant to exist. The students had set it up purely for their own entertainment.

Only the elite students, of course. And if Adam and Leo resented him and Slack for getting into Roy Lykos's classes, they were probably doubly annoyed about Salome inviting them to join their secret club. John grinned to himself as he opened the basement door and set off down the stairs with Slack on his heels. Adam and Leo might think they were the kings of the school, but he had plenty of non-homicidal ideas for dethroning them.

The stairwell here wasn't the sleek high-concept type; the steps and rails were plain steel, and John and Slack's footsteps sounded disconcertingly loud. This part of the school felt like the backstage of the theater of the Center itself: plain, utilitarian, *analog.* Hack Club's basement room was on the lowest level; beyond it there was nothing but a plain door with a lever bar. At this level, that couldn't be an emergency exit. John figured it was a cleaning closet, and since it never seemed to be accessed, Hack Club was safely private. As he and Slack opened the basement room door, Adam and Leo were already glaring at them.

<66>

Adam sat in front of a glowing screen; Leo stood behind him, leaning on Adam's chair.

"Ready to get your hides whupped, newbies?" asked Adam with a cold smile.

John opened his mouth to make some cutting retort, but the words got stuck in his throat. Light glared off Adam's hipster glasses, obscuring his eyes, and somehow that made him seem— just for a moment—less than human. Not that it unnerved John. Quite the reverse: he felt a tug inside him that was like a leftover from his earlier dream. Like he wanted to walk over to that desk and simply *delete* Adam.

John shook himself. *What am I thinking? They're just annoying nerds.* "Yeah," he said. "Go ahead and try, if you think you're up to it."

Behind them, the other club members were filtering into the room and shouting greetings and challenges, but John couldn't take his eyes off Adam Kruz. Even his white smile was *so* irritating.

"I'm gonna break your defenses so fast, backwoods boys." Adam flexed his typing fingers.

"Yeah," agreed Leo, his scowl at Slack deadly serious. "Might as well go order your pizza early, Hook. You haven't got a chance."

Delete him, too, thought John. He blinked in surprise at himself.

After all, the pre-fight banter between the Hack Club students seemed to be a tradition. Adam and Leo's version might have had an edge of real viciousness—but he didn't need to take it quite so personally, did he? There would be plenty of chances here to take down these two arrogant kids. He and Slack hadn't managed to do it over the past few Saturdays, but maybe today was their day.

<67>

"I'm Adam Kruz." The Russian-accented voice came from behind a screen farther back, and Eva Vygotsky rose to her feet, her black eyes sparkling with derision. "I'm not as smart as I think I am, but my daddy's Rick Kruz, so I think that makes me *very* smart. Hmph!"

It was not a bad impersonation, and John had to stifle a laugh. Eva wasn't laughing, though; she was eyeing Adam with mild contempt. John, intrigued, watched them both. Adam's father was Rick Kruz, the software developer, was he? No wonder the boy was so cocky. He must be worth a fortune.

Leo was glaring at Eva on his friend's behalf. "Yeah, Adam's dad invented Ubicomp; your dad, whoever he was, dumped you on a train. That's some competition."

The look Eva gave him was piercingly lethal. "I'll show you competition." She sat down and began to tap at her keyboard.

Salome, who had just entered the room, was watching the standoff nervously. In fact, the whole room had fallen silent; the back-and-forth had clearly gone way beyond normal rules. From the corner of his eye, John saw Slack take his phone from his pocket and tap the screen.

A resounding fart filled the air.

Leo Pallikaris's face went white, then crimson. The sound was coming from him. As it echoed over and over again, he fumbled for his phone, tugging it from his pocket. Finally, he stabbed the screen, silencing it.

The club erupted with laughter; only Adam and Leo stood in silence, filled with fury.

"Nice ringtone, Leo," said Slack. "If it is a ringtone?"

<68>

Leo jabbed a finger at him. "You're dead," he snarled. He yanked out a chair and set about typing furiously.

John gave Eva a smile, but she was ignoring everyone again, typing intently, the light of her screen flickering on her pale face. Salome, though, was studying him and Slack, and there wasn't nearly so much superior distaste on her face as usual. She was almost smiling, and John could have sworn she winked at Slack.

Maybe, as Mrs. Long would say, Adam and Leo aren't quite as popular as they think they are . . .

John sat down at his own screen and began to work.

<69>

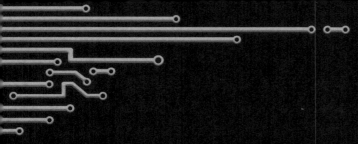

Ten

"Vygotsky!" Adam Kruz sprang to his feet. "You're going to regret that!"

Eva smirked at him. "Don't blame me for your poor peripheral vision, Adam Kruz."

"I never saw you sneaking up either," admitted Slack, kicking his chair back from the desk with a defeated grin. "That hack was a beauty."

"I was nowhere near getting through your firewall by the time you got through mine," said John admiringly.

Eva gave a shrug, rose from her chair, and marched out of the basement. They heard the tap of her boots as she ran lightly upstairs.

"She's so fast," sighed Salome, staring at the door through which Eva had vanished. "You know she just hijacked my system? That's how she did it. Look." She turned her screen to face John and Slack. "See? She launched her attack from here. And I didn't know about it till thirty seconds ago."

John leaned over. "She owned your whole system. You weren't having any effect at all?"

"I thought I was doing so well, but I've been a zombie for at least twenty minutes." Salome laughed. "I told you she was good."

"She's not that good," growled Leo, packing his laptop. "She's sneaky. You just weren't paying attention."

Salome sniffed. "Your jealousy is unbecoming," she told Leo and Adam. "'Sneaky' just means she's clever. Cleverer than you, by the look of it."

The pair left without another word while shooting venomous glares at Salome, John, and Slack. John couldn't help but laugh as the door slammed behind them.

"Touchy, aren't they?"

"They think a little too highly of themselves," said Salome. "You must have noticed that in class."

"Roy seems to like them," said Slack, "so they must be pretty good."

"Oh, they're *good*," Salome told him, "just not quite as good as they think they are. But they often beat Eva at Hack Club."

"Really?" Slack's eyes widened as the two boys followed Salome out of the basement.

Salome paused, a hand on the stairwell rail, and glanced at them. "Yes. Sometimes Eva seems to kind of . . . lose her way. She drifts off into another world, like she can't focus. Like she's forgotten everything. I think it's a condition, some kind of intermittent amnesia. And those boys take advantage. But there's another reason they get ahead of everyone. I'll let you in on a secret, if you can keep your mouths shut?"

The two boys nodded vigorously.

"Eva is convinced Adam and Leo get help from outside."

John gaped at her. "Outside? You mean from a teacher, or . . . "

<71>

"No. The teachers don't know about Hack Club." Salome headed for the smoothie bar. "Well, except for Roy. He knows it goes on, but he wouldn't help Adam and Leo. Why would he? They're two of his favorites. He wants them to get better, not to get by with cheating."

It was true, thought John: that wouldn't make sense. But if they weren't getting help from a staff member, how were they getting backup from beyond the school's security system? That didn't make sense either.

He shook his head. "But if they get help from outside . . . that would give any good hacker access to the school's system and files . . . "

"That is why they're idiots." Salome shrugged angrily. "But Eva's never found proof, and it's a serious allegation. She can't report it till she knows for sure."

Adam and Leo were lounging on beanbags at the other side of the broad hallway, basking in a patch of sunlight as they gnawed on pizza slices. Adam caught John's eye, and malevolence spread across his face.

"What's up, backwoods boy?"

John bristled. Adam had the nerve to call him names, when that kid himself was doing something so risky?

"Don't get involved, John!" whispered Salome, clutching his sleeve.

He shook off her hand and marched across to the two boys. "You can quit being so smug, since you're getting help from outside the school."

Adam rose to his feet and balled his fists. "Who told you that? It's a lie!" He glared over John's shoulder, in Salome's direction.

<72>

Instantly, John realized that Salome had been right: it was rash to confront Adam with no proof. He didn't even understand why he'd done it, except that something had clicked inside his brain. *What Salome says is true. And it's dangerous. They could let anyone in.*

But now hadn't been the time to bring it up. "Nobody told me," he said, backtracking fast. "I guessed."

"Now who's the liar?" Adam glared at Salome again, but then his eyes slid to Eva, who was slumped on a beanbag in the corner, her laptop propped on her knees. "It was Vygotsky, wasn't it? She can't stand that we beat her so often."

"It wasn't Eva," blurted John, wishing he hadn't said anything. It didn't matter that somewhere inside his brain, her accusation had been accepted. John might be the computer, but right now the computer was frozen, with a little spinning rainbow wheel where his thought process ought to be.

"Yes." Leo gave him a slow smile, his gaze flickering between John and Eva. "It is. Hey, Adam, it's time to play."

Adam glanced at him, nodded, and grinned. Both boys picked up their laptops and bags, turned on their heels, and strode away. Leo turned back to grab his last slice of pizza, and then they were gone.

"Shoot," murmured John.

"I told you not to get involved." Salome was at his side, her arms folded, stiff with annoyance.

"But it's true, what you said." John turned to her. "Isn't it?"

"I think so, yes. But you don't mess with Adam and Leo, not without evidence you can take to the teachers." Salome made

<73>

a face. "I'd double-check all your firewalls over the next few days, if I were you."

"I'll be caref—"

John was interrupted by a yelp of horror from the corner. Eva leaped from her beanbag, her laptop clutched in her hands. She stared at its screen, her black-rimmed eyes wide.

"Eva?" Salome hurried to her side. "What's wrong?"

Eva's knuckles were white, yet she didn't move. She was beyond *rigid*. She was absolutely motionless, except for her head. It jerked slightly, rhythmically.

"Eva?"

Eva's head stilled, and a shudder went through the rest of her body. She blinked as if she'd only just woken up; then, without a word, she turned the laptop to face Salome. Salome's face froze.

John and Slack walked over to join the two girls. "What's up?" asked Slack.

"This." Eva's face had gone even paler, if that was possible. "*This* is up."

A GIF of a grinning velociraptor filled the screen, instantly recognizable to anyone who'd seen *Jurassic Park*. Across it ran a line of repeating red text: *Clever Girl! Clever Girl!*

As they stared, aghast, the screen dissolved into pixels, then reassembled as lines of text way too heavy with exclamation marks.

OOPS!!!

YOU LOST YOUR FILES!!!!

MAYBE YOU NEED "OUTSIDE HELP"!!!

Better not rat even when your a clever girl!!!

<74>

And back came the velociraptor and its mocking tagline.

Eva tapped furiously at her touchpad, but nothing would shift the repeating message. Tears of frustration and rage brimmed in her eyes, but they didn't spill over.

"Oh no," whispered Slack.

Salome cleared her throat. "They can't spell 'you're,'" she said, with an attempt at a cheery smile.

Eva glared at her. "Don't you get it? I've lost *everything*."

John patted her shoulder. "It's OK, Eva. We'll help get your files back."

"You don't understand, do you?" She turned to him, glaring. "It's not just my files. If I can't fix this, *I'll lose my whole mind.*"

<75>

Eleven

There was no way she could be reading this. It must be a hallucination. Akane took a deep breath, rubbed her eyes, and very, very slowly read the email again.

She hadn't tried to fool any of the Wolf's Den directors: none of them would be clumsy enough to fall for even the subtlest phishing expedition. But the junior secretary who filed their records online—he'd been more gullible. Working through labyrinthine Chinese channels, Akane had posed convincingly as a corporate recruiter; once in possession of his password, she'd been amazed at how much of his employer's correspondence he'd left unprotected.

And now she wished she'd never looked.

Mr. Laine is very happy with the patient's progress but would like her to attend for further tests. Could you please call me to make arrangements as soon as possible?

I enclose his letter with this email.

I am pleased Akane is making such a good recovery!

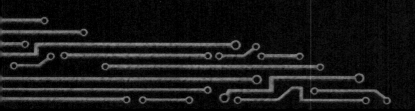

Akane's mouth felt dry. She wanted to swallow, but when she tried, there was only a high clicking sound.

She'd never been Mikael Laine's patient. She'd never hurt herself. She hadn't been born with some life-threatening condition.

Had she?

Maybe there was some other Akane Maezono. It was the most bizarre coincidence, but it was more likely than the other possibility.

But that's Papa's email address. It is.

Sagging forward, she pressed her forehead on the edge of the desk. It felt cool and sharp. *I have to look at the attachment. I have to.*

I don't want to.

Pushing herself back upright, she gritted her jaw. Her finger trembled over the touchpad, but at last, she stabbed it.

The letter wobbled and blurred in front of her eyes, as if her own retinas didn't want her to see this. But still it came through, word by insane word.

. . . Massive damage to the parietal and occipital lobes

. . . repair should not have been possible . . .

. . . however, I am extremely pleased with . . .

. . . remarkable response . . .

. . . continue to monitor . . .

. . . optimistic.

Optimistic.

Akane felt as if she were learning to read for the first time. Silently, her mouth formed each word as she read them over and

<77>

over again. There was no denying it. This had been written to her own parents.

She read the whole thing again, right down to the signature line.

Yours sincerely,

Mikael Laine

Akane realized she was trembling. Very carefully, she lifted her hand and touched her birthmark: that ridge of hard flesh under her hair.

"It's not a birthmark," she whispered out loud. "It's a scar."

A sharp rap on the door made her jump. "Akane?"

"I'm busy, Obaasan!"

She hadn't meant to sound so sharp, but funnily enough she didn't regret it. Her grandmother must have known about this all along. *She kept this from me too.*

Closing her eyes, Akane took deep breaths to calm herself. She didn't have time to meditate properly, but going through a few of the motions was enough. Cool determination flooded her, and at last she managed to stop the tremor in her fingers. Narrowing her eyes, she scrolled up to check the date of the letter again.

I was four. It's not surprising I don't remember. But why would her parents have kept this from her?

Akane typed and clicked furiously, digging up every email, every document, pausing only for a moment as the name *Jake Hook* slid past her eyes. She'd get back to John's new friend later. Because nothing about this was a coincidence anymore.

Maybe Okaasan and Otousan had had good reason not to tell her. Maybe they'd wanted her to forget forever that she thought she could fly. She swallowed, staring at one of her mother's

<78>

first emails to Laine. No wonder they didn't approve of her BASE-jumping antics: it seemed she'd started as a four-year-old, from the roof of the Gotokuji Temple.

Without a chute.

Akane scratched at her head. She let her fingertips dance across the ridge of her scar, then tugged nervously at her hair.

All of her friends had told her. They'd told her, every time she'd let them see it. *That's a weird birthmark, Akane.* And how she'd teased them. *Of course it's a special kind of birthmark, because I'm special!*

The email cache was scrolling down across her vision, almost unnoticed. Akane was barely paying attention, so she didn't know why one of them caught her eye so suddenly. But her finger stabbed the touchpad as she did a shocked double take.

Hi, Freki, yes. Experimental at this point, of course, but in the case of the Maezono child, I'm relatively confident.

Akane sucked in a breath.

If it does misfire, Mik, you understand that WD will be unable to take public responsibility. If you must know, I was unhappy with previous procedures which should have taken place under WD aegis. Control of subjects is not something to leave to chance.

WD? Who was WD? The tone of the email exchange was growing increasingly curt.

Not entirely happy with terminology, Freki, as I have clarified before. Children not property of WD.

Akane swallowed hard.

Mik. I repeat. Procedure is entirely property of WD, therefore subjects also.

<79>

Frantically, Akane scrolled up the thread. *Property? What procedure? What kind of medical intervention was the property of one individual, this WD?* The person Mikael was talking to didn't have those initials. It was just one name anyway. She looked at it again. *Freki.*

Maybe it wasn't a person's name at all. Maybe it was a corporation. Frowning, Akane typed the name into Google. The headline result popped up.

In Norse mythology, Geri and **Freki** (Old Norse, both meaning "the ravenous" or "greedy one") are two wolves which are said to accompany the god Odin.

With a grunt of impatience, Akane kicked her chair back. *Mythology! That doesn't help.*

Or did it? Wolves, she thought, her stomach sinking with dread. *Wolves . . . is that a coincidence?* John and Jake were in the Wolf's Den right now . . . Akane clicked back to another email thread. *Jake Hook procedure: details enclosed.* She barely dared to look. But she had to.

Thirty minutes later, she wished she hadn't.

How could Mikael Laine have dared to attempt something so experimental, on her or on Jake? Or maybe even his *own son?* But it had worked. Akane gulped hard. She would have died without his treatment. *I'd be long dead by now.*

The emails were full of medical jargon, but Akane could understand the gist of them.

There was something in her head that didn't belong there.

<80>

That casual mention of *genetically modified brain tissue* didn't sound human at all. What experimental matter had he used when he patched up her broken brain? *What was it doing to her?*

The fury and confusion were too much. Hurriedly pushing back her chair, Akane sprang to her feet and flung open the study door.

"Obaasan!"

Her grandmother turned from the stove, startled. Akane could only imagine how angry she looked; she didn't care.

"I have to talk to you! *Now!*"

<<>>

"Akane, you must understand." Obaasan shuffled back and forth across the wooden floor; if she hadn't been so small and wise, she'd have looked like an anxious, caged tiger. "Wait till your parents come home. You can ask them all about your accident, Akane-chan."

She looked almost desperate, but Akane hardened her heart. "They could have told me about it years ago, Obaasan."

"They didn't want to upset you or frighten you. Look how brave you are, Akane-chan! You're not afraid of anything!"

"No," she grunted, "and they stop me from doing *everything*. They grounded me the other day!"

"Are you surprised?" Her grandmother reached out to clasp her hands. "Jumping off buildings is what got you into this, Akane-chan!"

"I was four!" protested Akane. "And my sisters don't get grounded!"

<81>

Obaasan wagged a finger. "You are the youngest. They'd have been more protective of you, even if you hadn't—if you hadn't almost died." There were tears in her eyes.

"But I didn't die," whispered Akane.

"No, you didn't," nodded Obaasan. "They found a very clever brain surgeon, they told me. He saved you. And that's all that matters to your *haha* and *chichi* and to me."

Akane gulped hard. *But what did my parents let Mikael Laine do to me? Do they even know what he did?*

She rose and squeezed her grandmother's hands. It wasn't Obaasan's fault: she'd kept the secret, but it hadn't been her decision.

"I . . . I need to think for a while, Obaasan."

Relief flickered across her grandmother's face. "Your *haha* and *chichi* will be home in a few hours, Akane. They did what they thought was best. Don't be angry with them, please."

But they gave me to Mikael Laine without knowing what he would do. Akane took a deep breath. "I'll try."

"And don't look too much on your computer," the old woman pleaded. "I know the things you can find on that machine. You are clever that way, Akane-chan, but you should talk to your parents first."

Akane gave a short nod. But she had no intention of keeping that promise.

Back in her room, with the door firmly closed, she woke up the screen again. *Mikael Laine was a director of the Wolf's Den Center.* Cracking her knuckles, Akane opened Mikael Laine's file once more.

<82>

You clever man, she thought, as she studied his handsome, angular face. There was a hint of a shy smile on his wide-lipped mouth, as if he were teasing her. *Why did you disappear? Are you really dead?*

Anyway, I can be as clever as you.

She had a few hours, and that was more than enough. It was easy enough to track the correspondence that dated from Jake Hook's boating accident at the age of six, when the boom had struck his head and he'd been trapped under the water. *Let's have a look at your medical records, Jake . . .*

Her parents might be able to hide things from her, but no stranger was going to do the same. The InCubate Clinic ran a sophisticated IT system, but not quite sophisticated enough. Studying its hashed strings, Akane could already spot a weakness or two. *I've compromised fancier authentication systems before breakfast,* she thought.

John had been sent to the Wolf's Den. Jake had been sent to the Wolf's Den. They'd both suffered accidents that should have been fatal; they'd both been saved by Mikael Laine. And the connection between Mikael and the Center was right there in black and white in the list of directors, but that didn't tell her *why* he'd been involved. It certainly didn't tell her why the connection had been secret or why John had been kept in the dark about it.

What is John doing there?

<<>>

Checking the time, Akane sat back, releasing a breath. She'd scraped the Center and Clinic websites clean of information. That didn't mean there wasn't more to be had.

<83>

Entry points. Hmm. Medical: she'd done that.

Political? She didn't know her way around government sites the way John did, and she didn't want to get caught. Technical? Laine had kept his work well clear of legitimate scientific websites; she knew because she'd checked.

Legal . . . ?

There was silence next door as she worked, except for an occasional shuffle of slippered feet. At last she heard the television click on, the volume lower than usual. Clearly, her grandmother didn't dare disturb her. *Poor Obaasan.* It wasn't her fault, Akane reminded herself. She must be dreading what would happen when her son and daughter-in-law returned home . . .

Even that thought flew out of her head as the page she requested loaded.

The words floated in front of her, but she couldn't make sense of them. Maybe her brain didn't want to see the contract before her. Maybe deep down she didn't want to know about the agreement that bore those signatures, that agreement that assigned future rights in perpetuity.

Because how could you sell the rights to human beings?

Something cold washed over Akane. *Because maybe those human beings aren't human. Not anymore.* What had Freki said in that email?

"Procedure is entirely property of WD, therefore subjects also."

The law firm's legalese was complex and peppered with Latin, but this, too, Akane got the gist of well enough. Mikael had sold the rights to his medical procedure. More than that, he'd sold the rights to *her.* And John. And Jake. He'd sold them to the Wolf's Den.

<84>

The signatures were right there on the Crines, Macdonald, and Osborne website.

Mikael A Laine
Mikael Laine
[for InCubate Medical Group]

Yamamoto
Yasuo Yamamoto
[for Wolf's Den Center]

Akane couldn't move. Her bones were frozen. Her brain felt like a stranger's.

Then, in the distance, she heard the click of a key in the apartment lock.

"Akane? Mother?" Her father's voice drifted through, piercing the chrysalis of ice that seemed to have formed around her. "I'm home."

Once again, Akane let her fingers drift to her scar. She dug in her fingernails, hard enough to hurt, and gritted her teeth.

Then she kicked back her chair, stood up, and opened the door.

"Hello, Papa. We need to talk."

<85>

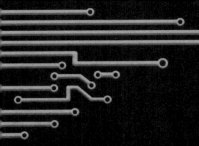

Twelve

John wasn't even surprised by the pool. He realized he was coming to expect the unusual as he flung himself in.

It wasn't the most elegant of dives, but he loved the sensation of hitting the water, of being swallowed up, submerged in silence. He swam down as far as he could. *You'd think the water's a little warm for those orcas, but it's fine for me.*

They slid past him through the water and disappeared from view, a pod of seven including a calf. John managed to touch his fingers to an outcrop of coral on the sea floor before kicking back upward. He gasped as he broke the surface and slicked back his long hair.

"Did you see the great white shark?" Only Eva was around; she sat on the pool's edge and squeezed water from her hair. Her voice sounded dull and monotone, like a tour guide who'd led a bus trip once too often.

"Aw, I must have missed it." John swam to her. "But this water's *definitely* too warm for those."

"*Carcharodon carcharias,*" said Eva flatly. "Able to smell a single drop of blood in a hundred gallons of water. May grow to up to

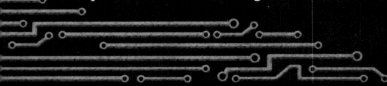

twenty-three feet and weigh more than six thousand pounds, of which 24 percent may consist of their liver alone. Preferred water temperature is fifty-nine to seventy-five degrees Fahrenheit; this pool is set to eighty-two degrees, but that doesn't bother Roy Lykos."

Hauling himself out of the water, John sat at her side and gave her a crooked smile. "Maybe you don't need to worry about losing your files. You seem to have them all in your head."

She was silent for a moment. "Maybe."

"I think this pool's even better than the climbing wall," he told her with forced cheer.

"It is a clever trick." She shrugged. "But then the Tiger-Father is a clever man."

"Who?"

"Lykos."

Wow, Eva was odd. John chewed his lip.

From up here the digital oceanic life wasn't visible; he could make out the glass screens that formed the sides of the pool, and they looked perfectly plain. *One day,* he thought, *I'll create things like this. I'll make them economically viable. I'll get them into every school in the country. But I won't be the one who had the idea . . .*

"He's brilliant," he said at last. "I know you don't like him, Eva, but I'm sure Roy could help with that malware on your computer."

"No. He cannot. And if he could, he would not."

John had no idea how to respond. Eva was frosty and curt and hard to talk to, but he couldn't help liking her. He ached with sympathy for what Leo and Adam had done to her laptop. But he liked Roy Lykos, too, and respected and admired him. Why did he have to be stuck in the middle?

<87>

He hadn't seen Eva look sad, or frightened, or vulnerable, in five whole weeks at the Center. Now she was all three, and she wasn't even trying to hide it.

He tilted his head. "What did you mean, you might lose your whole mind?"

"It doesn't matter what I meant. It's true, that's all."

"Can't you get another laptop? I know it's a pain, and you'll have lost all your data, but—"

"No!" Her head snapped round, and she glared at him. "That isn't an option, John Laine! You of all people should know that!"

"OK, OK." He slumped forward, leaning his elbows on his knees.

"They don't know what they've done," she whispered. "Stupid. Stupid. Stupid. Stu—"

She fell abruptly silent, her eyes glazing. John frowned and peered at her. She sounded unnervingly like a broken loop. "Are you—"

"Stupid. Stupid—" Her eyes brightened again with fury, and she spoke as if he'd never interrupted her. "Stupid little rich boys. They have *no idea*."

Eva didn't sound like an automaton anymore. She sounded so angry that John wasn't surprised that her shoulders began to shake. He was much more shocked when he realized she was actually crying. Silent tears slid down her cheeks even as she glared at the rippling pool.

"Oh, Eva. It'll be OK; I promise." Nervously, John put a comforting arm around her, and she didn't shake him off. "We'll fix it. Me and Slack and Salome, we'll find a way."

<88>

"Thank you." Abruptly she pressed her face into his shoulder. "You are the only ones who can help."

"We're not," he said, risking a smile, "but you won't go to Roy, so . . . "

She ignored that. "You will keep my mind intact. You are my friends; I trust you."

"Uh . . . good. That's good." Her complete trust made him feel even more protective. *Not something I ever guessed I'd feel toward Eva Vygotsky* . . . "You want to swim again? It'll take your mind off it for a few minutes."

"My mind needs to keep its focus," she told him seriously. "But, yes, a swim will not affect that, and it may help. You are kind, John Laine." She scrambled to her feet. "And after all, *these* are only digital sharks."

John watched her leap into the water. After a moment, he, too, stood up, rubbing his arms.

Why had he found her last remark so unsettling? Was it the tone of her voice or her emphasis?

He shook himself and plunged head-first after her. *Maybe this time I'll get lucky and see the great white.* It wasn't as if it would bother him.

After all: these are only digital sharks.

<<>>

Beads of sweat broke out on John's forehead. Maybe computing was harder physical work than climbing or swimming after all. He didn't have time to test for comparison: he was perched on a bench in the gym, but instead of lifting weights, he was hammering at his laptop.

<89>

Guilt ate at him. He should never have confronted Adam and Leo; he was the reason they'd done this to Eva. He'd been battling the malware on her computer for days now, and he hadn't made any progress. Slack had been trying too, and Salome, but none of them could make a dent in the program.

It wasn't as if Adam and Leo had made any demands. This was pure revenge—a warning to Eva not to rat them out again and a threat of worse if she dared to tell any of the teachers. There was no sign of them relenting, either.

Salome, being Salome, had tried pleading with their better natures. She'd used all the reasoning and logic that served her well in Roy's classes, but it hadn't done any good. All Adam and Leo would say was, "We'll think about it." Then Adam would wave a regal, dismissive hand, and they'd walk off together, giggling.

With a growl of frustration, John pushed his laptop away. It almost shot off the bench, and he had to snatch it out of thin air before it hit the mat.

"No luck?" Salome grunted, letting the barbell clang back onto its rest and sitting up.

"Nothing," said John. "I thought I'd found an inversion pathway to get me back to their start point, but it hit a dead end. You're right: they *are* good."

"Only in a technical sense," said Salome dryly. "Why don't you lift some weights? Or go on the cross-trainer. Work off some frustration, like Jake's doing."

John glanced through the plate glass to the next room. Slack had been beating a punching bag to death for forty-five minutes, and there was no sign of him letting up. His jaws were clenched

<90>

tightly, and he was drenched in sweat, but still he relentlessly hammered at the punching bag.

John took a deep breath. "I don't think it's working for him, but I'll give it a shot."

"A break and some physical activity will help your brain."

"Sure. I'll try again later with Eva's malware."

"We all will."

"Salome." John hesitated. "I tried to ask her, but she wouldn't tell me. What did Eva mean, she'll *lose her mind*? Is it something to do with her amnesia?"

Salome shrugged and strode to the weights rack to grab another couple of plates. Methodically, she began to screw them onto the barbell. "I don't think so. She's not actually mad or anything. Eva's odd, that's all, and that laptop is her life. She didn't mean it *literally*."

John wasn't so sure, but he didn't like to say that out loud. "I wish we could help her. She's so frustrated and miserable." He stretched his shoulders. "She can't focus in class. Even Yasuo laid into her yesterday when she froze, and you know how easygoing he is."

"We could try telling Roy Lykos," suggested Salome. "He'd help."

"No! Eva won't hear of it—and she's right. You know what Adam and Leo said yesterday—they can do a lot worse. I wouldn't put it past them to delete all her files permanently."

"Horrible, spoiled brats," exclaimed Salome, slamming the lock onto the barbell plates with emphasis. "That's what a rich daddy does for you."

"Your dad's rich."

<91>

"Not half as wealthy as Rick Kruz. And my father didn't bring me up to believe the world should bow to me. According to my dad, we owe the world, not the other way round." Salome snorted. "I'd love to see those two spoiled children get their comeuppance."

It was unlike Salome to sound so vindictive, but John didn't blame her. The Ethiopian girl took pride in seeing the best in everyone; her faith in humanity was touching, even if he and Slack did mock it a little. She must be *really* angry with Adam and Leo, because she seemed to have demoted them from her list of Worthwhile Human Beings. *Horrible, spoiled brats* was not the worst thing John had heard her call them in the past few days.

Still, he could hardly judge her. That nightmare about killing Adam and Leo had turned into a recurring one. His subconscious seemed to find it cathartic, because he got a lot of satisfaction from the dreams while he was in them. He actually *enjoyed* turning those boys into shattered pixels.

But the six o'clock alarm was always an awful moment. Every morning he awoke, sweating, completely convinced he was a real, live murderer.

"You look tired." Salome narrowed her eyes at him. "Are you getting enough sleep?"

"'Course," he lied.

"Mm-hm." Salome didn't sound convinced.

Stubbornly, John climbed onto the cross-trainer to prove how energetic he felt. The computerized screen blinked to life as he clasped the sensors.

John Laine is on the cross-trainer, it greeted him cheerfully. **Hello John Laine! Four mile run? Yes/No**

<92>

"The classes feel pretty intense in your first few weeks," Salome pointed out. "Especially Roy's. You could be forgiven for being, y'know, *exhausted*."

"Yeah, but I'm not." John stabbed the screen aggressively. *No.* He prodded the panel. *Five.*

Five mile run, 6 mph Yes/No

No. 7.5.

Five miles, 7.5 mph Welcome John Laine!

The small screen seemed to swell and widen, enveloping him; the words dissolved into an image of a rough track that wound through green hills.

Grimly, John began to stride, but his legs already felt wobbly and weak. By the time the digital track rose toward a distant mountain, he was gasping for breath; after less than half a mile, he gave up. As he leaned on the rails, panting, the screen shrank, and the digital illusion disappeared.

"I thought so." Flopping back on the bench, Salome rolled her eyes toward him. "Go and get some rest, John. *Now.*"

There was no point in arguing with Salome in this mood. She could be annoyingly maternal, but John was secretly relieved to be given the order. Tucking his laptop under his arm, he left the gym.

The atrium was busy as usual, most of the tables and pods occupied by late-lunching students, and John wasn't feeling sociable, so he headed up the sloping walkway toward the dormitory wing.

Sunlight spilled through the glass roof, giving him a powerful urge to get outside and let the Arctic air clear his mind. *But I*

<93>

haven't got time. I don't have time for anything but this wretched malware.

Resentfully, he slouched on toward his room. Ahead and to his right was the short corridor that led to Yasuo's garden-office; John wished he had a space like that. With a calm and light-filled working area, he might at last find the perspective he needed to fix Eva's bug.

Temptation nudged him into the corridor. What was it Roy had said? *Yasuo always has time for students.* Not to mention space—Yasuo often let favored students use the calm circular room for study. *He wouldn't mind . . .* If Yasuo wasn't there, there was nothing—not even a door—to stop John from borrowing it for half an hour. And that gravel garden might be downright inspiring . . .

Slowing, he edged along the corridor. No, shoot. Yasuo *was* in his office: John could hear his voice.

Actually, he could hear an argument. *Wow, the teachers fight? Even Yasuo?*

John craned his ears. The clipped German accent was instantly recognizable.

"—I will not hear of it. Lykos has no right."

John's eyes widened. He'd never heard anyone refer to Roy quite so contemptuously and only by his surname.

Yasuo's calm tones floated from the office. "Take a moment to consider, Irma. More flies are caught with honey, as the Americans say."

"The *flies* are already caught," she snapped. "We have been in possession of them for six weeks and five days, and they are *not* Lykos's to do with as he wishes."

<94>

"I was speaking of Roy," he said patiently. "Let him indulge his methods. It might even keep him conveniently busy. What harm can he do?"

"Extreme harm, Yasuo, as you are well aware. The subjects are secure here, and testing is well underway. It would be madness to let Lykos play with the programming, if programming it is. He is capable of far too much mischief, and worse, he has a predisposition for it." She took a sharp, audible breath. "I do not trust him. I would sooner see Project 31 destroyed than to have him interfere."

The hair on John's neck raised. What did Ms. Reiffelt have against Roy Lykos? He'd known she was severe and scary, but he hadn't realized she could sound so vindictive.

Yasuo sighed. "Roy is very dedicated to his students."

"Too dedicated." Her tone was venomous.

"Roy knows you are monitoring him, Irma," soothed Yasuo. "He will not risk anything that could have him removed from this facility."

"I wouldn't be so sure." Her voice lowered till John could barely hear it. "He could ruin everything, Yasuo. And I do mean *everything.*"

Slowly, John backed away. He was afraid to hear another word. What was Irma Reiffelt planning against Roy? What *project* would she rather destroy than have him involved?

Backing out of the corridor, John hurried toward his and Slack's room. He hadn't thought it was possible to feel sorry for someone as wealthy, successful, and brilliant as Roy Lykos, but if Irma Reiffelt had it in for him, he didn't envy the man at all. *Poor guy.*

<95>

With a sigh of relief, John slumped onto his bed. Staff room politics were no different here, it seemed, and he was mighty glad the two teachers didn't know he'd overheard.

It was funny, though, he thought with a smile. Whatever the *flies* were, they'd been at this facility for six weeks and five days.

Which was a coincidence, since that was exactly the same as he and Slack.

<96>

Thirteen

There was no question of taking a nap. John sat cross-
legged against his pillow and opened his laptop again. How could
any self-respecting hacker sleep with this challenge nagging at
his or her brain?

Yet he'd run out of ideas. It was good to think outside the box,
but he'd turned left, right, up, and down, and he didn't know
where to try next. John scowled at the lines of code he'd uselessly
typed in earlier.

I could kill Adam and Leo.

No. He blinked, shocked. He didn't really mean that.

Put it this way: I'd like to wipe them off the Matrix.

No. No, no, no. It was their *program* that had to be eliminated,
not them. They were stupid, arrogant kids—that was all.

They're a virus.

NO.

John tossed his laptop onto the quilt. He was shaking.

This was the feeling he got in his dreams: this thrill of homicidal longing. It didn't belong in his head while he was *awake*.

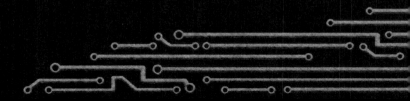

It wasn't only in his head, either. It rippled through his bones, an urge to get up right now, to walk to Adam and Leo's shared room, and to delete the malware at its source.

"Oh, that's *it*," he exclaimed out loud. Jumping down off the bed, he shook his head violently. Maybe he did need some physical exercise.

Grabbing his jacket, he headed for the stairwell that led up to the plateau. The blast of cold wind that hit him as he emerged was like a healthy slap in the face.

There was a layer of fresh snow. Picking a direction at random, he walked till he reached the precipitous cliffs and sat down with his legs dangling over the edge. He took a few deep breaths of the clear air. Even the fleece-lined jacket that kept the Fairbanks chill away wasn't very efficient on Little Diomede, and John realized he was shivering, but it didn't bother him. It took his mind off that tingle of hatred in his blood.

Across the gray sea lay Big Diomede, gloomy and desolate under heavy cloud cover. It looked like some sinister island Odysseus might visit, or maybe the Prospero's Isle. *It's tomorrow over there. Maybe, where it's tomorrow, I've already solved Eva's problem.*

Far below, surging waves crashed against the rocks; across the water, a smear of darkness between sea and sky told him that more snow was falling out there. Winter was definitely approaching in earnest.

John closed his eyes and tilted his face upward, letting the north wind whip his hair across it. This beat the gym, the climbing wall, and even the wild oceanic pool. He felt better already. Maybe his grandfather had a point about the benefits of fresh air . . .

His phone bleated in his pocket.

<98>

Startled, John glanced to the left and right, but there was no one in sight. He tugged the phone from his pocket. Something about the message tone sounded wrong, somehow, yet it was familiar.

Then he realized. It was the call of a Japanese bush warbler. It was the ringtone he'd set for Akane.

His heart leapt as he opened his messages. How was this even possible? Out here there was no signal from his home provider, and the island's Wi-Fi network was supposed to block any outside calls. Yet there was Akane's cartoon face, smiling from beneath straight black fringe.

Can you talk?

He glanced over his shoulder, then tapped the screen eagerly. *Yes.*

OK. FaceTime now.

By the time he'd tapped the FaceTime icon, the real-life Akane was already there. This Akane's smile had an edge of tension, and her eyes looked strained.

"John!"

"Hey, Akane! You've no idea how glad I am to see you."

"*Same*," she told him emphatically. "John, is everything all right over there?"

"It's . . . great," he told her truthfully. "Mostly."

"Good. I . . . I was worried about you."

"Why?"

"There's no . . . well, nothing strikes you as off about the place? Nothing odd?"

John shook his head. "No, it's fine, Akane. It's good."

Even on the small screen, he saw her sag with relief. "Oh, thank goodness. I couldn't get in touch with you. All my messages bounced."

<99>

"Well, that's the only thing." He wrinkled his nose. "We don't get outside contact, which is a pain."

"That's been bugging me."

"I hate that part, but it's for security. There's so much hacking going on, all legitimate and supervised, and I guess they don't want to risk some outside sneaker getting in through a back door."

"Fair enough." There was something guarded in Akane's voice.

"It begs the question, though. How *did* you get in touch?"

She grinned, looking for the first time like the old devil-may-care Akane. "You know the accelerometer inside your phone?"

"Yes . . . "

"I used electromagnetic radiation to detect what you've been typing. That let me declassify your whole online footprint. I got in that way."

John gave her a broad grin of delight. "Clever girl . . . " His face fell as he realized he was echoing Adam and Leo's ransomware. "I mean, nice one. When did you think of . . . " His brow furrowed. "Wait a minute—"

"I've got a confession to make." Akane looked guilty. "I've been tracking you for a while."

John stared at her. "What, like you told me *not* to do to you, ever again?"

"Sorry." She chewed her lip.

"I never noticed. Why didn't I notice?"

"I was really sneaky. Sorry. And you weren't expecting it, I guess."

"That's how you caught on to Slack's hack so fast. Back in Fairbanks, I mean."

"Yeah. Sorry again." She took a deep breath. "I was worried about you. I . . . look, John, your dad had gone missing, and he

<100>

wasn't there to protect you. And you were so distracted, and . . . I was worried," she finished, lamely.

Akane had been monitoring him, and he hadn't known about it. *I didn't pay enough attention. Dad was right.* Fleetingly, John felt a twinge of hurt.

Along with it, though, came a strange and detached sensation: a cold calculation in his brain, as if a background program was already running. *Fix that bug.*

Catching his breath, John shook his head. "Don't worry. I'm glad you did, now. But Akane, can you keep contact to a minimum right now? We shouldn't be doing this."

"OK."

"Because I'd be in big trouble if the teachers found out."

"Oh, I'm sure of it." Her eyes darkened.

"What's that mean?"

"Nothing," she said quickly. "I mean, I'd like to talk to you properly, John. There's stuff we need to discuss. I've dug up some . . . odd files. Bizarre ones. But if this isn't a good time . . . "

His eyes shifted to the time at the top of the screen, and he made a face. "It's not. I've got to be in class with Ms. Reiffelt in six minutes, and *nobody* is late for her classes."

"I'll bet."

John frowned. "How d'you—why would you say that?"

Akane blushed. "I might've . . . " She cleared her throat. "I might've looked at the staff profiles."

John laughed out loud. "You're brilliant."

"I know. You know Reiffelt used to be an East German spy?"

"Yep. Except she wasn't; I asked Yasuo. She was a double agent. That's how she ended up here."

<101>

Akane gave him a long, intent look. "*Here*. A canoe ride away from the Russian border."

John shook his head. "No way. That's a coincidence. Yasuo says she got into IT really early, but she saw right away how much faster it was developing in the West. So she defected and started working for them. For *us*."

"Hmm." Akane narrowed her eyes. "Doesn't sound like she was a conviction convert."

"But she was," insisted John. "At least half the research at this school is for big corporations." There was no time to tell Akane about the conversation he'd overheard, but it had sounded like Ms. Reiffelt was as fiercely competitive as any good capitalist. "Listen, I really can't talk right now. She'll have me in detention if I'm a millisecond late. She's scary. But also, her classes are *great*. I have to go!"

"I'll get in touch again, John," Akane said, with a hint of urgency. "We *must* talk. You're sure you're OK?"

"Positive." John scrambled to his feet. "But this has been great. Laterz, Akane!"

Only when he'd pressed disconnect and tucked his phone back into his pocket did John remember he hadn't told his best friend about the malware attack.

Never mind. It can wait. He shrugged and jogged back toward the Center, his heart much lighter now. He was still a little annoyed about Akane's secret tracking hack, but that was more his fault than hers. And it had been so good to talk to someone on the outside—especially when that person was Akane.

She might have some ideas for fixing Eva's malware, something I just haven't thought of. He'd talk to Akane again soon, and together they'd come up with a way to kill that bug.

It really is the only thing that's wrong around here.

<102>

Fourteen

Shivering, Akane stared at the blank FaceTime screen.
John sounds fine. Everything sounds great.

I know it isn't.

Beneath the shade of the Gotokuji maple trees, Akane set down her backpack and studied the clustered, happy white cat statuettes. The *maneki-neko* by the shrine were a serene sight, shining and cheerful, and she'd needed something to calm her down.

What she *really* needed, of course, was a flight through cold air. A plunge at terminal velocity might clear her head . . . but after that awful confrontation with her mother and father, when she'd demanded answers about her childhood accident and operation, her BASE-jumping equipment had been confiscated altogether. Ironically, the argument had made her parents even more determined to keep her feet on the ground.

You must see now why we're worried! You still have that reckless streak, Akane . . .

Her father had been remorseful about the secrecy, even a little apologetic, but he had sternly defended it. *We hoped you would forget jumping. You were a daredevil even then. But we did not want to make our brave daughter afraid. You have to put yourself in our place. Our beloved child was back, and the horror was all over!*

And when her mother had come home, not ten minutes later, she had been just as firm. *It was better that you didn't know. Your accident, it was best forgotten by all of us. I'm sorry if your feelings are hurt, Akane, but we thought it was for the best. We don't know how Mikael Laine did it, but he saved you.*

And the really annoying thing was that Akane *did* understand. When they'd hidden her accident from her, her parents had done what they had to do. They'd tried to shield her from the consequences of her own actions. She'd only been four years old, after all.

Now, with her parents at work and a BASE jump out of the question, Gotokuji had been the only alternative outing that Obaasan would agree to. Akane had had to swear on her honor that she'd go straight to the temple gardens and back, with no dangerous detours. But she didn't truly mind: Gotokuji Temple had seemed the natural place to retreat to. After all, this was where it had all begun.

This is where I decided to fly from the temple roof. This is where I nearly died.

This is where I began to become the property of the Wolf 's Den Center.

The gardens were beautifully quiet, but even though Akane had peace to think, it was difficult. Golden leaves stirred in the breeze, and puffy clouds glowed pink in the late sunlight, but she could hardly focus on calming her breathing.

<104>

It had been impossible to tell John everything in that phone call. He'd been in a hurry, and she hadn't had time to explain properly, and besides, a stolen and hurried chat hadn't seemed right for such a momentous conversation.

She had to try again. *What else can I do? I have to tell John what I've found out.*

But for all Akane knew, a secret call to John might be detected and monitored. What kind of trouble might she get John into?

He should know his father set up the Center with this Freki person, she reminded herself sternly. *And John should know what's been done to him. What's been done to me too.*

She had to find a way of telling him; Akane just couldn't think what it was. And it was going to take a lot of tactful explaining, and it wasn't as if she could just get on a plane and go to Alaska.

Branches dipped in the gentle breeze. Leaves whispered and rustled. She could hear the hum and bustle of the city in the distance. A footstep shuffled on the path beyond the trees.

A what?

It was only a footstep, on a path, in the middle of a tourist attraction, so Akane didn't know why her whole body suddenly tensed, why every sense was raised to high alert. She focused her ears on the low voices.

"She came in here." It was a soft murmur.

"Then find her," said another voice.

Akane's heart raced. She backed very slowly away from the cats and deeper into the shadows of the trees.

The first voice spoke again. "I thought this one was to be harvested next term?"

<105>

"Schedule's been moved up. There was a security breach this morning. Hold on, let me listen to this message from the Center."

Shutting her eyes tight, Akane swore at herself. *Of course* there would have been a trip wire programmed into the files. *Of course* they'd know if a hacker intruded. She'd been so eager, so hungry for information, that she hadn't bothered to watch out for booby traps and disable them, or even to cover her digital tracks on the way out. She hadn't thought about blocking the inversion pathways.

You idiot! she berated herself. What kind of trouble had she attracted? Hacking medical records, legal files . . . but now wasn't the time to worry about it.

Above her head there was a sturdy, smooth branch; Akane sprang up silently to grab it and hoisted herself into the tree. Peering out between the leaves, she could see them: two dark-suited men, with slick hair and cold eyes. One of them had a phone to his ear; the other idly scanned the gardens as he waited.

They didn't look like police.

Several long moments passed as Akane crouched rigidly among the branches. *She came in here,* the one with the cellphone had said. There was no one else close by, so they had to be talking about Akane. Besides, her instincts were bristling, and she always trusted those. What did those men want with her?

"This is a tricky one," said the man with the phone, pocketing it. "We need to do it quietly. They don't want a fuss."

Do it quietly? thought Akane. Her stomach lurched.

<106>

His colleague slipped a pair of mirrored sunglasses over his eyes. "What about her parents? The grandmother?"

"We can get her out of the country quickly. The important thing is to get her to the Center. They'll handle it from there. There's nothing the family can do if they don't know where she is."

Akane could barely breathe. Get her out of the country? Without her parents' consent? Sure, she'd hacked the correspondence, the medical records, and that awful contract. But this . . . it seemed extreme . . .

Procedure is entirely property of WD, therefore subjects also . . .

A hideous memory flashed in her brain: it was one she'd filed in the back because she'd been so preoccupied with the medical procedure and the legal contract. But she thought of it now.

It was the file named Defense Applications.

Akane's mind whirled, racing. If the Center owned her and John and Jake, there had to be a reason. Who owned the rights to something they couldn't use?

Defense Applications.

Akane hadn't asked herself before, but she did now: *What are we for?*

What are we actually for?

And what do I know that I shouldn't?

Would these men kill her? No, that was ridiculous. Why take her all the way to Alaska just to dispose of a body? And, anyway, Akane thought with a fearful shiver of disgust, she was a valuable piece of property.

But if they got her to the Wolf's Den, she could easily vanish: just another missing person. Her parents would search, but they

<107>

wouldn't find her. *I'd be completely under the control of my . . . owners.* Akane shuddered again and had to grab a branch to keep her balance. This one was slender: it bounced, and the leaves shook and rustled loudly.

Both men glanced up. The one with the sunglasses stepped forward.

"Maezono-san?"

Akane cursed herself. There was no more time to think. She leaped to the ground, landed with a grunt, and ran.

"Maezono-san! Akane! We only want to talk!" She ignored their shouts. Bolting through the trees, her backpack jolting against her spine, she tried to think. *They know where I live. They'll follow. They'll find me.*

So in that case, why had they bothered to follow her to Gotokuji? *Because they want to do this quietly. Just take me. They won't take me from my house.* She knew it with a sudden, powerful surge of hope: it would be too risky for them, too overt. *If I can just get back to the apartment—!*

Gotokuji was a quiet place, secluded, shaded by so many trees. It was peaceful, and when she'd come here, she'd done exactly what they wanted; they probably couldn't believe their luck. Home might be safe. But to get home, she still had to get out of here . . .

A bolt of fear shot through Akane's gut. Panting, she darted and dodged through the trees and sprinted down another walkway. If she'd had any doubts, any vague hope that she was imagining things and being overly dramatic, they'd vanished; she could hear the men's swift running footsteps behind her, their leather soles scraping the stone pathway.

<108>

The setting sun was dazzling, peeking through the branches and dappling the mossy ground, half blinding her and making it hard to orient herself. But Akane kept running, racing in a wide circle through the trees. Her pursuers were fast, she realized with a surge of panic, and they weren't tiring.

Ahead and to her left she caught sight of the tall wooden pagoda, and she sprinted toward it; then, darting suddenly to the right, she plunged in among the memorial stones and statues of the cemetery.

Ducking behind a thick pillar of stone, she halted, panting. Despair filled her chest. *This is useless. Even if I get out of here, they'll find me somewhere, somehow.*

No. I won't just give up! If she could just get home, it would give her breathing space. Enough time to make her own plan . . .

If I can just lose them here!

Akane stiffened, holding her breath. Quiet footsteps were treading along the stones and methodically covering the ground. They might take a little while to find her hiding place, but eventually, they would.

Gripping her pack straps, taking a deep breath, Akane leaped to her feet.

Sunglasses was to her left, six rows away; Cellphone was right ahead of her, just one line along. Their heads spun toward her, and Cellphone gave a shout of triumph. They must have split up to cover more ground. Just as well, then, that she loved parkour . . .

The stones were tall, all straight-sided pillars and obelisks, but a lot of them had flat tops. Springing up onto the nearest one, Akane leaped lightly to the next and then to the next.

<109>

Cellphone rushed for her and grabbed at her ankle, his fingers brushing the hem of her jeans. But he missed and swore, and she leaped on in nimble strides.

They were after her again, fast and intent, but she didn't glance back. She kept jumping and leaping, praying she wouldn't fall, inwardly begging forgiveness from the dead as she ran in great bounding steps across their stones and back toward the temple.

As she jumped down from the last pillar and bolted back into the gardens, Sunglasses gave a shout of frustration and dodged clumsily around a statue after her. *I'm ahead, I'm ahead . . .*

Her heart lurched in panic. Cellphone was nowhere in sight. *Where is he?*

Akane tried to swivel her head as she ran, searching desperately for a second running shadow. As she pounded gasping through the trees and toward the temple, she at last caught sight of him; the two of them had split up again, trying another two-pronged attack. Cellphone had circled the trees, and now he was running toward her, from the other side of the temple.

Akane skidded to a halt on the grass, and for a horrible moment she hesitated, agonizingly torn. The men were closing in on her. She swung toward one, then the other. There was nowhere to go but the temple itself, and if she ran there, she'd be trapped—

Clenching her teeth, Akane darted through the temple gateway.

"Got her!" she heard Sunglasses yell.

Ignoring him, she sprinted through the small courtyard. Grabbing one of the wooden pillars at the temple's corners, she

<110>

yanked herself up and scrambled hand over hand onto the roof. At its edge she crouched, staring back down at the men.

Cellphone halted, glaring up at her. Then he swore, grabbed a pillar, and began to climb. He wasn't as agile as she was, but he looked strong. He was going to be up where she was at any moment—and Sunglasses was following his example, moving rapidly up another pillar.

Turning, Akane ran again, up the low slanting roof and down toward its far edge. Over the clanging of her feet, she could still hear the men's shouts, but she didn't hesitate. She drew a deep breath—

For the second time in her life, Akane took a flying leap from the roof of the Gotokuji Temple. But she was not four this time, and she didn't have time to be afraid. The ground rushed up to meet her, and air rushed into her lungs, making her give a high-pitched gasp. Pain jolted through her as she landed on her feet with a grunt. Then she sprang up and bolted along the walkway to the main gate. As she stumbled out of the gardens, she gave a cry of triumph and terror.

Beyond the entranceway, the narrow streets were lined with shops; Akane had never been so glad to see real, live pedestrians. She hurtled between them, dodging bags and elbows, and she did not stop running till she was lost in the crowds at Miyanoza-ka Station. When she finally dared to look over her shoulder, there was no sign of Sunglasses and Cellphone. Sucking in deep breaths, she tried to calm her trembling limbs and whispered a quick prayer of gratitude to the temple cats.

Thank you, maneki-neko. You brought me luck.

Now I just have to build on it . . .

<111>

What was it she'd told herself, as she stared at the temple cats and agonized about getting her information to John? *I can't just get on a plane . . .*

The temporary safety of the apartment felt like a blissful haven; all the way home, Akane kept glancing over her shoulder, terrified that Cellphone and Sunglasses would loom out of the crowds. Her parents and Obaasan must have thought she was crazy: she rarely gave them such fierce, desperate hugs as she did when she rushed through the front door.

But she was still in danger, Akane knew. And so were they. She'd bought a temporary reprieve, and Cellphone and Sunglasses wouldn't launch an attack on her home—not yet, at least. But when would their employers run out of patience?

Quietly, firmly, Akane closed the door of her study, dumped her backpack in the corner, and flipped open her laptop. Her limbs were still trembling, and her fingers felt numb. From the kitchen her mother was calling out to her, but supper could wait.

Akane swallowed hard. Minimizing the window that held the Wolf's Den files, she opened her browser.

"What are you looking for, Akane?"

Her heart tripped and thudded. Drat that thing. She'd forgotten she'd personalized that robotic voice. With a glance toward the door, she muted the volume and tapped out her request the old-fashioned way into the search box.

"Get me to Alaska."

<112>

Fifteen

Obaasan had stopped going to the market altogether in the mornings. Instead, Mrs. Hagashi had taken to popping over more often to gossip. Which meant there were now two pairs of beady old eyes watching her.

Akane was desperate for Mrs. Hagashi to leave, but there was no rushing her grandmother's morning news broadcast. She'd have to wait, that was all, and pass the time by going over and over her own medical files, and John's, and Slack's.

She'd thought she'd found the vital information, but that was before she'd started delving into the detailed biological records. How could something so terrifying be so fascinating?

Biology wasn't her specialty, but with focus and diligence, Akane could almost see how it had worked. How it *still* worked.

And once she had a grasp of what Mikael had done, and how he had done it, she began to see *why* it had succeeded. It was genius, she had to admit. And if biology wasn't her forte, the other aspects of this procedure certainly were. Akane furrowed her brow as she read intently. There were so many links to follow, so many pathways to investigate. Every way she turned, she

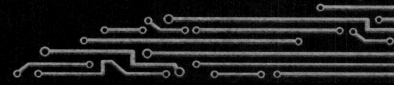

found another intriguing diversion into the cellular process and how it kept her alive.

By *intriguing* she really meant *frightening*. But then, Akane reminded herself, she'd never been scared too easily. With a grin she glanced back at her chute, and at just that moment, she heard Mrs. Hagashi's cheery "*Mata ne!*" and the door of the apartment clicked shut.

Akane sprang to her feet. Now or never . . . Obaasan was puttering in the kitchen area, rinsing porcelain cups and reorganizing her enormous collection of herbal teas. Akane tiptoed up behind her and squeezed the old woman's waist.

"Akane!" She turned and smiled. "I thought you were busy with your computer?"

"I was, but I've got something to tell you, Obaasan." Akane gave her grandmother her most innocent, wide-eyed smile. "How does a vacation sound?"

"A vacation?" The old woman's eyes creased.

"You know you like to travel," said Akane. "You *loved* Singapore and L.A."

"Yes, yes, I did." Obaasan drew back a little and frowned at her. "What's that got to do with anything?"

Akane took a deep breath and whipped a printout from her pocket. "We're going to Alaska!"

"We're going *where?*"

"Alaska," said Akane. She pushed the paper into her grandmother's tiny hands.

Frowning, Obaasan reached for her glasses and peered at the printout. Her eyes flickered as she read the words over, slowly and carefully. "A competition?"

<114>

"Yes!"

"You won this trip?"

"*Yes.*" There was no need for the old woman to know that she'd hacked her way into the winning draw at japanlovealaska.com. It had been so easy that Akane was almost embarrassed. *But it's for a good cause.*

"Alaska," said Obaasan faintly. "Akane-chan, you know why I liked Singapore and Los Angeles, don't you? I like *cities.* I like shopping and coffee bars and theaters and—"

"Alaska is *beautiful,*" Akane told her firmly. "Come and look at my computer and I'll show you photos."

"Alaska is *cold,*" pointed out her grandmother. "And *bleak.*"

"It's not bleak at all," said Akane. "Anchorage! Fairbanks! They're cities! And you can see the aurora borealis. And reindeer. Polar bears!"

There was a wistful light in Obaasan's eyes as she bit her lip. "I've never seen the northern lights . . . "

"No, and they're supposed to be amazing!"

Obaasan peered again at the piece of paper. "And you really won this?"

"I really did. And the trip is for two people!"

"It would have to be," said Obaasan dryly. "Your parents would forbid you to go alone. In fact, I'm not even sure—"

"If you talk to them, Obaasan, they'll let me go," pleaded Akane. "*Please?* I've always wanted to see Alaska!"

The lie went unnoticed, thank goodness, and the old woman nodded slowly. "Let me think about it, Akane-chan . . . "

"That's the thing." Akane bit her lip hard. "There's not really that much *time* to think. The flights are, uh . . . soon."

<115>

"How soon?" Obaasan narrowed her old eyes.

"Like, in a couple of days?" Akane put on her most winsome expression. *It's not like I could leave it till next month. And besides, the website might catch on to my hack in less than a week . . .* "Oh, please, Obaasan? Okaa-chan and Otou-chan won't be able to get time off work. You're my only hope."

The old woman gave a great, defeated sigh. "Well, if you *promise* not to go jumping off any mountains, I'll ask them." Her grandmother took her hands and gazed solemnly into her eyes. "None of this case-jumping thing."

"BASE jumping. And there's not a single skyscraper in Fairbanks," Akane said evasively, "as far as I can see on Google Maps."

"All right. All right, I'm willing to ask your parents if you're sure you'll be good."

Akane nodded eagerly. It wasn't as if she'd told her grandmother any *huge* lies.

After all, Obaasan hadn't asked straight out if she was going to head for an island in the wilderness, seek out John Laine, and investigate the murky dealings of a sinister cyber-organization . . .

Akane felt the way she did when she stood on the edge of a high building, her toes inching out over the abyss. There was a thrill of adrenalin in her bloodstream, a mounting excitement churning in her gut. She was on the verge of a leap into the unknown, with a singing awareness and understanding waiting for her out there—if she dared to make the plunge.

All I have to do is jump.

<116>

Sixteen

John was on the verge of something; he could feel it.
All I have to do is—

No. He didn't know what he had to do.

With a muttered curse, he flopped back against the chair and stared at his laptop screen. He had settled himself in one of the small study rooms on the lower floor of the west wing; it was a little cramped, but unlike his own room, it was completely free of distractions like that tempting 3-D gaming console. There was nothing here but a desk, a swivel chair, the hum of the air-conditioning, and his own laptop.

But even that single screen was maddening. Lines of code flickered and scrolled across it, mocking him. This malware shouldn't be so hard to combat. It *wasn't* that hard; he knew it in his bones—if he could only find the hidden gate he knew was there, that elusive little tunnel of code that would take him to the digital heart of that stupid, *stupid* velociraptor. He wanted very badly to stab it right in the chest.

John shook himself. His violent dreams were more than enough to cope with, and they'd been getting increasingly worse.

He certainly didn't need to feed that thrill by fantasizing about killing things while he was awake—especially since he tried to be awake more and more of the time. His dreams while he was asleep were way too disturbing.

Apart from anything else, his father would disapprove—even of the imaginary killing of a pixelated dinosaur. John gritted his teeth and pulled the laptop back toward him. But he knew how to fight this malware. He shouldn't be this frustrated in the first place. *What would Dad tell me to do right now?*

Closing his eyes, he pictured Mikael's face in his mind. It had been getting harder to do that, but now he forced himself to focus. Akane would know how to do this. *Clear your thoughts,* she'd say. *Empty your mind. Concentrate on one thing only.*

Piece by piece, he reassembled his father's features in his mind's eye. Clear gray eyes. A craggy face, crinkled by smile lines. Dark blond hair swept back from his forehead. Squeezing his eyes tighter, John focused on bringing all the elements together.

There he is.

John found himself smiling. His father had always had a stubborn look, despite his laughing eyes—there was a light of determination in their depths. That was how Mikael had dealt with problems like John's: by doggedly returning to them, over and over again, even when it seemed hopeless. *Sometimes you've already hit on the answer.* John could hear his father's voice quite clearly. *You've just missed the one small thing that will make the difference.*

A single line of code. A single letter, even. *Look long enough and there's nothing that can hide from you. Just look.* Mikael had been endlessly patient and tenacious.

<118>

Opening his eyes, John blinked at the laptop screen and took a deep breath. His fingers drifted back to the keys, and he began to type. The pathway was one he'd tried before, but he felt a tingle of renewed curiosity. It was as if he'd gone back to it by some underlying instinct.

The bug had a pattern of behavior. They all did. *Swim with it, John.*

He dived into cyberspace, his fingers flying across the keyboard. The bug had been redirected multiple times, bouncing wildly around the world like a crazy, blind bluebottle fly. But that didn't mean the original IP address didn't have significance. John looked again.

It seemed to buzz ahead of him like a will-o'-the-wisp, constantly out of reach—but for the first time he could *see it.* Only its afterburner, maybe, an imprint of light on the back of his eye, but he knew it was there. Fixing all his attention on that trail, John followed it. *I know you! I see you!*

His fingertips were working by themselves now. Information flew at him from all directions, but that didn't bother him. It was as if there was another John standing alongside him, batting the irrelevant data away, catching hold of the true stuff. Parallel John swept a hand across a screenful of data, shattering it into nothing; then he snatched a fistful of code and reshaped it, filtering it into Real John's brain. Real John typed like a madman.

Certainty seeped into his brain: *This is where I belong. Cyberspace. This is my home.* His father had guided him here. That made sense—of course it did. He could see his dad's face clearly once again.

<119>

Ironically, it was his mom's face that wouldn't form now. Because *this* was his mother: this world, this time and space. His home was *everywhere.*

So many Johns seemed to be in control of him: John who selected the data, John who struck the keyboard with the precision and speed of a concert pianist, and Real John who fused it all together. And it was working. He was nearly there, nearly there, and the zipping comet tail of the malware was almost within his grasp—

"John! *John!*"

The urgent voice shattered the illusion, and a violent physical jolt almost sent him flying. Lines of code shattered like glass in his head, and he jerked back from the laptop and gasped.

Salome had kicked his chair hard away from the desk. John panted, gripping the edge of the desk and trying to reorient himself.

"What's going on?" demanded Slack.

"He looked like he was possessed." Salome's face appeared close to his, peering into his eyes. "Were you possessed, John?"

John blinked hard, about to shake his head. Instead he found himself giving a single, sharp nod.

"Well, that would explain a lot." Slack, now propped against the desk, rolled his eyes. "Seriously, though. You were totally on another planet."

John, finally getting his breath and his balance back, gave a strangled laugh. "You're not kidding. That was weird."

Salome frowned and folded her arms. "I've heard of getting caught up in your work, but that was ridiculous. Your fingers were going so fast they were *blurred.*

<120>

"We must have said your name six or seven times. Didn't you hear?"

John shook his head.

"You need more sleep," she told him sternly.

"That is probably true." He sighed. "I just felt like I was getting close, and I didn't want to stop." It was the only explanation he could think of for the odd fugue state—and certainly the only way to describe it to Salome and Slack without sounding like a lunatic. He felt a tug of regret about being yanked away from what Slack called *another planet*, but not as much as he'd have expected. *I can find that bug again now. I'm sure of it.*

At least all those multiple Johns were now safely back in his own head and under control. He shivered slightly. "Anyone for pizza?"

"No more junk food, Laine," scolded Salome. "It's a kale smoothie for you. You're going to start looking after yourself better."

John rolled his eyes, but he grinned. "It's like I have three mothers."

"Three?" She gave him a quizzical look.

"Two. I mean, two." John felt a flush cover his cheekbones. What was he talking about?

One thing was reassuring: he could bring his mom's face to mind again just perfectly. That odd moment of sensing another ghost-mother seemed to have passed.

"A smoothie for John, a pizza for me, and then the gym," suggested Slack. "I'm not drinking mushed kale for anybody, not even—" he started. "Eva?"

<121>

John swiveled his chair around to face her. The girl had appeared at the door of their room, her black-rimmed eyes wide and alarmed.

"John. Jake. Salome." She gave each of them a sharp nod. "The Shark Twins are coming."

"The Shark Twins?" asked Slack. "And I wish you'd call me Slack."

"Very well, Jake."

"She means Adam and Leo," explained Salome, sounding nervous. "Let's go."

"And the Tiger-Father. He is coming too."

"She means Roy," explained John to the others.

"Because he's like one of those Tiger Moms."

"No," Eva contradicted him with a sharp look.

"Because of tiger sharks." As John blinked in surprise, she turned from one to the other, her face expectant. "I think we do not want him to know what you're doing."

"No, we don't," agreed John with feeling. "I'm with you there. I trust Roy, but Adam and Leo have made it clear they'll wipe your files if we tell him anything."

"Never mind the Shark Twins," she said. "I would not tell Lykos anyway."

John was about to argue, but Eva's unsettling stare had grown even more intense. Shrugging, he quickly closed his laptop and packed it away.

"Those boys are always around when you least want them," complained Slack as they left the little room and closed the door. "It's like they have a sixth sense."

<122>

"Why are they coming *here*?" asked John irritably. As they turned the corner toward the atrium, he saw Eva's warning had been exactly right: Adam and Leo were there in front of them. The two boys stopped short, glowering, as John and his friends pushed past.

"Troublemakers," hissed Adam.

"Troubleshooters," Slack corrected him, with a cold and cocky smile.

With an impatient snap of her fingers, Salome hurried them along, until they were out of sight of the Shark Twins. "Don't antagonize them," she told Slack. "I bet we haven't seen their worst yet."

"We have not," said Eva. "I'm sure of this."

"Never mind that just now." John reached for Eva's hand and squeezed it as they entered the atrium, earning a surprised look from Salome.

"What's going on?"

It was always a calm, light-filled space, but right now there was a buzz of energy and activity. Nobody was playing with holograms or concentrating on three-dimensional chess pieces projected onto the tables. The atrium was full of students who hurried in the same direction, clutching bags and laptops, their expressions urgent and nervous. John realized almost immediately what else had changed: the sliding ceiling had been closed. No Arctic sunshine spilled down from above; the only light came from brilliant circular LEDs on the walls.

One person was not among the moving mass. Roy Lykos sat at one of the abandoned tables, a laptop open in front of him. His light blue eyes rose to meet John's, but his expression didn't

<123>

change; it was one of calm but intense concern. He didn't even blink.

"I sense a disturbance in the Force," drawled Slack.

For once John didn't laugh. "What's gotten into everybody?"

Across the broad floor marched Irma Reiffelt, her steely eyes riveted on Salome, Eva, John, and Slack. Without breaking stride, she clapped her hands briskly.

"Where have you four been? Whole-school meeting in the basketball court. Immediately."

<124>

Seventeen

Every single student was here, John was sure of it.
There was still an impatient crowd in the atrium, but there was a
logjam where the corridor narrowed past the room that held the
weights, the treadmills, and the cross-trainers. The murmurs of
unease had swelled to a loud muttering and were turning into
loud, mutinous chatter as the crowd was forced to wait. Above it
all, the teachers shouted instructions and reassurance.

"This won't take long."

"Please proceed to the basketball court. *No shoving, please.*"

"Keep calm but go as quickly as you can. No, Chima, you may
not return for your laptop. No, nothing is that important. Deal
with it later."

Close to the corridor entrance, laptop bags and cases were
stacking up. John saw two girls at the head of the line pause, then
hand over their laptop cases to Imogen Black, who added them
to the pile.

"Where's Eva gone?" Slack turned, frowning; the girl had
slipped away. But as John glanced around too, Slack edged closer
to him. "Wait, what? They're taking everyone's computers."

"Why?" Disbelieving, John eyed Imogen as she put up a stern hand to stop two boys in their tracks. Both shrugged and handed over their laptops. "Why would they do that?"

"John. John." Salome's urgent whisper reached his ears at last, and she tugged on his T-shirt sleeve. "*John.* Look!"

She was pointing through the plate glass window of the weight room as they shuffled slowly past it. John's eyes widened.

He could see only two of the cross-trainers' display screens. Ordinarily, he'd have had to squint hard from here to make out the detail. But the image on them now was instantly recognizable, even at a much lower resolution.

It was a grinning velociraptor.

"No!" he said. "That's the ransomware—"

Salome jerked a thumb at the neatly stacked laptops. "It's spread," she said grimly. "It must have infected the whole school. That would explain why they're confiscating laptops."

"And phones," muttered Slack, nodding toward the basketball court doorway. Now that they were closer, John could see it was true: the Malware Defense teacher, Howard McAuliffe, was opposite Imogen and holding a plastic crate in his arms. Students paused, reluctantly dropping in their smartphones.

"But we only use them for games anyway!" came Lee Minseo's mournful cry. "They're not connected to the internet. You checked mine yourself!"

"Doesn't matter," said McAuliffe sternly. "Any device has potential to be hijacked to access the mainframe. Turn them over. Next!"

Ms. Reiffelt was pacing up and down the line ahead, her hands behind her back. "Until the malware problem is resolved," John

<126>

heard her say, "there will be no digital activity from anyone. It's important to quarantine all infected devices. The staff will work as fast as possible to clear this bug, but in the meantime all students are confined to the court. Your devices will be returned to you as soon as possible."

"I don't believe this," groaned Slack. "It's a school for geeks! They can't take our phones away!"

"It won't be for long," Salome told him uncertainly. She clenched and unclenched her fists as if she was already itching for her keyboard. "I'm sure Ms. Reiffelt and the others will sort this out soon."

"Why are they putting us in basketball jail, though?" Slack demanded. "Why not just send us to our rooms?"

"Because we could access the school's mainframe through the gaming consoles," John pointed out miserably. "Through anything with a screen and an input, basically. I guess they want to stop any more computers getting infected."

Slack pointed back at the cross-trainers. "It looks to me like there aren't *any* unaffected computers."

"What a mess," groaned Salome.

John clenched his jaw. "We don't know how long this is going to take. That bug is a beast. I've got to get a message to Akane."

"You can't do that!" Salome looked horrified.

"I can try. My phone was fine twenty minutes ago, and Akane showed me a communication channel."

"Give her my love," grinned Slack, with a raise of his eyebrows.

"Oh, for heaven's sake." Salome's shoulders sagged. "Well, *be quick*. And don't let any teachers see you!" She glanced anxiously

<127>

around. "Give me your laptop bag. There's no way you should be opening that."

"Fine." With a resigned sigh, John handed it to her.

"And I'm not kidding." Salome peered ahead at Ms. Reiffelt, who was launching once more into her monotone speech for a new batch of students lining up. "*Hurry.*"

Ducking his head, John wriggled through the sea of bodies. There was an alcove not far back, an L-shaped recess that held an emergency landline. Checking for any teachers who might be watching, he took a breath and dodged into the small space, then scuttled into the corner between the wall and the clunky phone.

He pulled his smartphone from his pocket, and the screen lit up. Hurriedly, he shielded it with his hand.

He'd already poised a finger to unlock it when he realized that wouldn't be necessary. The lock screen wasn't there. He gasped, his heart frozen. Instead of his screensaver, instead of the keypad for his PIN, there were two shimmering, flashing green words.

GET OUT.

In his disbelief, John couldn't move. He could only watch the words pulse and gleam, burning themselves onto his eyeballs. **GET OUT.**

John tried to swallow. They'd hacked him already. Those two vicious creeps had targeted his phone. *His* phone. Because as realization horribly crept into his brain, he knew what was missing from this particular bug: the velociraptor.

It was a different hack, one made especially for him.

GET OUT.

Adam and Leo detested him just for being here. They hated that he'd made it to Roy's class on day one and even more that

<128>

Salome had invited him to their precious Hack Club. Those rich little spoiled *brats*—

John slumped back in despair. The palm of his hand glowed green where the words flashed against it. Angrily, he clicked the off button to send the screen to sleep.

It didn't work. The words still pulsed at him, urgent and intense.

GET OUT.

John stabbed at the off button over and over again, but nothing would shift that display. He glared at it, his head buzzing with the words. He could *feel* them, deep inside his brain: their aggressive syllables, the hard edges of the letters. They bounced and rebounded, multiplying till the inside of his skull felt like a screenful of code. And the oddest thing of all was that they felt like they belonged.

This software is compatible.

And just like that, the words on his phone altered—dissolved, shattered, reformed. This time they were red.

GET OUT. NOW.

John leapt to his feet. He barged out into the corridor and fought his way through the crowd of students, ignoring their angry protests. He stumbled on someone's shoe, caught himself in time, and shoved onward, pushing people aside.

Where are they? I'm going to kill them—

He glanced toward the basketball court. Adam and Leo weren't there. He didn't know *how* he knew that, but he could sense Parallel John again, dismissing the crowded court with a sweep of his hand. Real John turned and began to run back along the line of students as he headed for the atrium.

<129>

He slowed as he approached the end of the corridor, his heart beating hard with fury. He couldn't be seen by a teacher; he'd be sent back to the line, and he'd miss his chance to delete the two human bugs.

This time, John ignored his own savage feelings; instead of wincing, he simply brushed the thought aside—for now. Edging against the wall, he peered cautiously around the corner.

There they were. And why weren't Adam and Leo in line for digital quarantine like the rest of the school? The two boys stood at the end of a passageway at the north side of the atrium, their heads inclined slightly. Leo nodded once. They were listening to someone inside the passageway, someone John couldn't see.

As quietly as possible, John stepped out into the atrium and up onto one of the glowing walkways that circled it. Adam half glanced over his shoulder, as if he'd heard something, and John went still. Then the boy returned to his conversation.

John sidled up the western walkway around the atrium, keeping close to the polished sandstone wall. The light from the LED fittings was not nearly as revealing as the usual pale sunshine; it cast odd but useful shadows. He couldn't risk running, but he crept as fast as he could around the vast space, keeping one eye on the two figures below, dodging into doorways whenever they seemed about to turn. Only when he'd reached a point directly opposite them did he stop and back into a shallow recess. Now he could see the little group clearly.

He could see who the two boys were talking to. His heart rattled with shock.

It was Roy Lykos.

<130>

Eighteen

The distant hubbub in the gym corridor had faded to almost nothing; most of the students were by now in the basketball court. John knew he was running out of time. Soon the doors would close and the teachers would begin to count off names, and they'd know he was missing.

Well, so are Adam and Leo.

John crept with agonizing caution around the high eastern walkway, all the way back down the length of the atrium. His feet silent on the blue glowing glass, he darted from shadow to shadow until he was almost above the three murmuring figures. A few more feet, and he'd be close enough to make out their words. *It's probably about their test scores*, John reminded himself sharply. *Roy's taken them aside to give them a talking to. That's all.*

But why now, when the school was in quarantine and practically a state of emergency? It was beyond bizarre.

Almost breaking into a run, John darted the last few steps to another recess and shrank inside it, breathing hard. The murmuring echo below resolved into actual words.

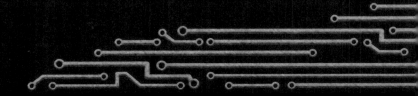

"It wasn't good enough." That was Roy's voice, acerbic and disapproving. "Do you know how close he came? That's what triggered this shutdown."

"Sorry, Roy," whispered Adam.

That's what triggered this shutdown. What had those two idiots been up to? John wouldn't have thought they had the imagination to cause this disaster. No wonder Roy Lykos was furious.

" . . . stupid and reckless," spouted Roy's voice again. "Now get out of my sight. I'm disappointed in you both."

So this mysterious meeting was just a tongue-lashing for two fools from a senior tutor. Almost disappointed, John grinned ruefully at his own sense of drama.

But it was good news, he realized with a rush of relief: if Roy now knew what had caused the mass infection, he could fix it. Maybe the quarantine wouldn't last too long after all.

Adam and Leo scuttled off in the direction of the gym wing, their shoulders hunched. John clenched his teeth. Now he could follow them back and confront them. If he'd been a bit afraid of them before, with their slick designer clothes and their arrogant sneers, he certainly wasn't now: they looked thoroughly chastened. He couldn't wait to tell them what he thought of them—

John hesitated and glanced down. Roy Lykos had stepped out of the passageway; his cropped head was directly below. Nervously, John peered over the railings. *I can't go while he's there.*

Would Roy head for the basketball court with the others? Maybe not. More than likely he was going to work on the bug. So once Roy headed for the mainframe computer in the east wing, John could sprint down the walkway and get to the basketball court before the teachers noticed—

<132>

John froze. Roy wasn't going to the east wing. He was walking purposefully toward the stairs that led to the basement.

That did not compute. There was nothing down there but the abandoned storeroom where Hack Club met.

At the back of his brain, John felt a tingle of urgent curiosity. When the basement door closed softly behind Roy, he burst from where he was hiding and ran down the walkway after him.

Breathing hard, he eased the basement door open and slipped inside. The lights on the stairwell burned lower than usual, maybe because the power was being diverted. But in the shadows far below, he could see the foreshortened figure of Roy Lykos as he turned into the farthest passageway. The man didn't even pause at the Hack Club door; he walked on toward the end, to that plain, lever-barred cleaning cupboard door.

Roy shoved down the bar, pushed the heavy door open, and slammed it behind him.

John's blood pulsed in his ears as he hurried down the stairs. It wasn't so easy to be quiet on the metal steps, and he was afraid of any faint ringing echo. *I'm like Theseus in the Labyrinth*, he thought with nervous amusement; *maybe I should leave a trail of thread to guide me back out.*

What on earth was he thinking? He should be back with the others by now, having his name on the register ticked off and waiting dutifully for the all clear to be given. What made him think he should be tracking a software superstar into the bowels of a secret cyber-complex?

His brain did, that was what. It was like a command being typed repeatedly inside his head, and there was no resisting a logical urge.

<133>

It's not logical.

Yes, it is.

You're just being nosy.

Parallel John flicked away the nagging voice of sense and conscience, and Real John, grinning in approval, jogged lightly down the remaining steps.

He crept quietly along the passageway and paused at the end, his heart throbbing. Doors like this, with a clanking bar lock, were horribly noisy to open. Cautiously, and with infinite slowness, John pressed the bar down. His fingers trembled, and when the lock gave its last loud jolt, he almost jumped out of his skin. For an instant he froze, terrified he'd been heard.

But the door gave way. It wasn't a cleaning cupboard. It opened into a sleek, brightly lit corridor.

Roy was already out of sight, but there was only one way he could have gone. The far door, across the corridor, wasn't old style or lever barred; it was smooth and plain, with a small plaque and a glowing security pad.

John hesitated, one hand still clutching the door. He wasn't Theseus in search of a minotaur. He was Lucy in the Wardrobe of Narnia, he thought with a sudden, nervous grin. And what had Lucy always been told?

He pulled his phone out of his pocket, ignoring the glowing bug on its screen, and crouched to wedge it between the door and the wall. *Always leave the Wardrobe door open.*

Straightening, he stared at the door ahead of him. Its brushed-chromed plaque told John nothing. In embossed sans-serif digits, it simply said 31.

<134>

There were no other rooms. There wasn't a 30 or a 32.

31. The number tingled in his brain. From the files running in his brain's background, one popped out, and he remembered.

Project 31. The one Irma Reiffelt would rather see destroyed than meddled with by Roy Lykos. 31. *Flies and honey. Six weeks and five days.*

The buzzing in his brain was almost a roaring alarm now. Clenching his jaw, John pressed his right palm to the security pad. He didn't really expect his nano implant to work, and sure enough, the glowing rejection appeared immediately: ACCESS DENIED.

He frowned. What about the iris recognition software that controlled his own dormitory door? It was worth a try. John peered into the screen, and it brightened.

DEVICE NOT COMPATIBLE.

ACCESS DENIED.

That was that, then. He was hardly going to knock and call Roy's name. In that instant, the burning curiosity faded and blinked out, like a window on a screen being closed. Simultaneously John thought: *I'm in trouble if I don't get back NOW.*

He ran for the emergency door, snatching up his phone and slipping back through before it clanked shut. He hurried along the passageway past Hack Club and onto the stairs—he took them two at a time, his breath coming hard and fast. *I should've spent more time on that cross-trainer . . .*

He reached the top of the stairs and flung open the basement door.

And almost collided with Irma Reiffelt.

<<>>

<135>

For a moment Ms. Reiffelt simply stood there, so rigid she almost quivered. Her eyes behind her slanted glasses were bright with shock, but as John watched, they turned cold and hard as granite.

"What do you think you are *doing*?" Her voice shattered the silence like an ice pick.

"I . . . " John swallowed past an obstruction in his throat. Ms. Reiffelt was shorter than him, almost as small as Eva Vygotsky. But he'd never been so petrified in his life. "I was looking for . . . Eva," he gasped at last, with a flash of inspiration. "I didn't see her in the line, and I thought . . . "

"Eva Vygotsky," said Ms. Reiffelt, her tone clipped and cold, "is in the basketball court with the rest of the school. Where *you* should be. Right now."

He really was in Narnia; he felt as if he'd been turned to stone. John would have sworn he could feel ice crystals forming on his eyelashes. "I . . . uh . . . oh."

"Go there. Immediately."

John darted past Ms. Reiffelt, mumbling apologies, but was brought up short by her voice once more.

"Your phone."

"What?"

"Your phone." She extended a hand, palm upward. Her fingernails were clipped short, John noticed, but painted a gleaming silvery gray. "All devices are to be temporarily surrendered."

Honestly, she was like a public service announcement, probably in some bleak authoritarian state. But she was hardly likely to frisk him. Was she?

<136>

"I . . . I gave it to Mr. McAuliffe. Howard, I gave it to him already."

Ms. Reiffelt stared at him for a long moment, her eyes as metallic and cold as her nail polish.

Why did I just lie? Why did I do that? He had no idea whether she believed him, and his heart was about to slam its way through his ribcage.

"Very well." Ms. Reiffelt jerked her head. "Go."

Faster than he'd even thought possible, John went.

<137>

Nineteen

"This is such a lovely surprise. John's online friend!
I can't tell you how happy I am that you came to visit." Tina Laine
smiled at Akane. "I wish John had told me more about you, but
it's so good to meet you! I'm just sorry he isn't here right now."

"I'm sorry too," said Akane. "But it's so nice to meet you, Mrs.
Laine."

There was no need to tell Tina that she'd known all along that
John wouldn't be home. *With a bit of luck I'll see him soon anyway.
If I can work out some way to do it . . .*

She and Obaasan sat side by side in Tina's spacious living
room, a glass of Coke in Akane's hands and a cup of coffee in
her grandmother's. John's home was bigger than Akane had
expected, a sprawling modern ranch house, and—fortunately
for Obaasan—it was toasty-warm inside. The old woman had at
last discarded her puffy winter jacket, and her face was pink with
excitement as she enthused about her unexpected holiday.

"I never thought I would see the northern lights," she told
Tina. "So beautiful! And we went to the Ice Museum, didn't we,
Akane? And Pioneer Park and the botanical garden . . ."

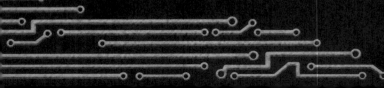

There was no need to make stilted conversation while Obaas-an was here, thought Akane affectionately. Her grandmother had never gone to an expensive international school like Akane, but thanks to her travel bug in her younger days, Obaasan's English was almost as good as her own. And though Obaasan had been a little bemused at the "multitude of attractions" Akane had eagerly advertised, she would never be anything but polite to her Alaskan host.

Letting her grandmother chatter, Akane studied the room. The prints on the walls were impressionistic landscapes, all bleak, snowy mountains and wild swirls of aurora. Statuettes of caribou and calves stood on the mantelpiece, as well as carved ornamental horns; of course, thought Akane, John's grandfather was a caribou herder. It must have been quite a change of lifestyle for the family when they'd moved north from Vancouver to live with him.

Framed photos stood on the corner table beside her. There was John, with his father on a trip to the United States, the distinctive Seattle skyline clear in the background. Akane squinted at the picture. She recognized Mikael more easily than John himself, who was a serious, chubby-faced child of about six or seven. Mikael wore a white T-shirt and a flannel shirt, and his smile was broad. Otherwise, he looked no different from the profile photos on his Wolf's Den dossier.

A lot happier, maybe . . .

"That's John's father." Tina's voice broke into her thoughts, and Akane realized she'd been staring too intently. Tina was smiling, though. "His name was Mikael."

"Was?" said Obaasan, blinking. "Oh, I am so sorry."

<139>

Tina nodded. "Thank you. It was very hard for John. He and Mikael were so close when he was little." Looking wistful, she pushed back her dark hair. "Mikael was much too busy with work for a few years before he died, but John still pretty much hero-worshipped him."

"It is so sad for a boy to lose his father. What was his work?" asked Obaasan.

"He was a neurosurgeon," said Tina with pride. "A pioneering one."

Akane was starting to feel guilty and more than a little nervous about where the conversation was going. Obaasan hadn't known the name of the surgeon who saved her granddaughter; when Akane had asked her whether they could visit her friend John's family, she very deliberately hadn't mentioned that connection. And Akane certainly hadn't let on to Tina Laine that she herself had been one of her husband's patients.

"John's a brilliant computer student," she interrupted brightly.

"He really is," laughed Tina. "He got his scientific brain from his father, I think. My specialty's English literature."

"Oh, I do *love* William Shakespeare!" exclaimed Obaasan, and she was off again.

Akane breathed a silent sigh of relief. Her Coke trembled in her hand, and she set it down. "May I use the bathroom, Mrs. Laine?" she asked as her grandmother paused for breath.

"Of course, Akane!" Tina turned her head and yelled from the living room. "Oh, good, Leona's home. She'll show you where it is. Leona! Come and meet our guests!"

The girl who entered the room was only three years older than she was, Akane knew, but she looked a lot more sophisticated.

<140>

Her hair was glossy, beautifully styled, and the same almost-black as John's and Tina's. She wore lipstick and eyeliner that were expertly applied, and her clothes were boho-chic. As introductions were made, Akane felt downright intimidated. It wasn't a feeling she was used to.

"You're John's online buddy?" asked Leona, tilting her head. "From Japan? Wow. Anyway, come on and I'll show you where the bathroom is."

Ugh, this was frustrating. All the same, Akane smiled. *It's not like I should be snooping anyway. I don't even know what I'm looking for.* "Thank you, Leona."

As they passed through the doorway and Leona led her along the hall, Akane noticed that the girl was giving her a hard sidelong examination.

"You do this hacking stuff with John?" asked Leona at last. "That's what got him into trouble, you know."

"I know," Akane sighed. "But that wasn't with me. I think he was led astray by that friend of his. They got up to some bad stuff together."

"Oh, Jake Hook." Leona rolled her eyes. "He's even more annoying than my little brother."

"John's not annoying," protested Akane.

"You don't have to live with him." Leona gave a dramatic sigh. "But, yeah, OK. Actually, he's mostly in his room with that wretched laptop, doing stupid stuff."

Akane bit her tongue.

"Anyway," said Leona, rounding a corner and pointing to a door, "there's the bathroom."

"Thank you."

<141>

Leona didn't leave, though. She propped herself against the wall and twisted a strand of hair between her fingers. "I'm glad you're here," she blurted.

"Really?" Akane blinked. "I mean, uh . . . thanks . . . "

"Yeah." Leona glanced furtively back toward the living room and lowered her voice. "You're staying here tonight, right? That's good, 'cause I need to ask you something. I'm worried."

Akane opened her mouth, then closed it again. "Huh?"

Leona leaned closer. "Later, OK? When Mom and your grandma have gone to bed."

"Sure, I—"

"We need to talk," the older girl said. Suddenly, she sounded a lot more serious. "We need to talk about John."

If Leona had some weird idea that she was romancing her younger brother, thought Akane, she did *not* want to talk about it. Whether it was going to be cozy big-sister advice or stern older-teenager warnings, she was *so* not interested. So she felt a lot less guilty about leaving Leona in the lurch than she did about the rest of this plan.

The house was silent and pretty much full of darkness. She'd waited long enough to be sure of that. Swinging her legs out of bed, holding her breath, Akane strained her ears again. Even when a floorboard creaked loudly beneath her, there was no sound in response. Her heart thumping, Akane pulled on her boots and jacket and lifted her backpack. No need to get changed; never intending to stay asleep all night, she'd gone to bed fully dressed.

That thing some women had, about showing you around their whole house, was a useful tradition, Akane thought mischievously.

<142>

She knew exactly where she was going. The utility room was in a small built-on extension at the back of the house, and when Tina had proudly shown her the dryer and the new washing machine (mothers, honestly), Akane had taken note of the open window. The gap had been filled with cobwebs; it must have been wedged open permanently to let the steam out. Akane grinned to herself. *Easy.*

Laying her note neatly on the pillow, then closing the bedroom door, she felt a twinge of guilt. Obaasan would be so worried. But there was no way her grandmother would agree to a detour all the way to the Seward Peninsula, hundreds of miles to the west. Akane's trip would take a few days, that was all: she could only hope that, though Obaasan would undoubtedly call her parents, they wouldn't alert the Alaskan police quite yet. They were more than used to their daughter's reckless sense of adventure, after all.

She'd never hitchhiked before, but there'd been a time—longer ago than she'd realized, to be fair—when she'd never jumped off a building, either. All she had to do was get to Anchorage, then catch the park service bus—

Oh, who was she kidding? Akane swallowed hard. Breaking the journey down in her head, she wasn't sure she was going to get away with any of this. Of *course* Obaasan would call her parents, and of *course* they'd alert the police. It was a five-hundred-mile trip, at least, and Akane would be lucky to get ten miles before she heard the wail of a siren.

But what choice did she have? Sunglasses and Cellphone were out there somewhere, hunting for her, and they probably weren't the only ones. John had been out of contact now for more than

<143>

twenty-four hours, and her hack of his phone had been disabled. She had to try.

No, "There is no try!"

She was halfway down the stairs when she heard the click of a latch.

"*Akane!*" It was an urgent whisper, not a yell of horror. A shape stood in the darkness on the landing.

"Leona." Her heart plummeted as the older girl hurried down the stairs to her side.

"Where are you going?" hissed Leona.

Akane's throat felt as cobwebby as that utility room window. "I . . . Leona, please, please don't tell. I have to find John."

Leona stared at her, her blue eyes almost glowing in the darkness. Without her makeup she looked younger and a lot more vulnerable.

"I know," she whispered at last. "That's why I wanted to talk to you. Come with me."

"There," said the older girl, pointing at the screen of the desktop computer.

John's bedroom was filled with moonlit darkness. There was a single iron bed with a patchwork quilt and a reindeer-skin throw, a chair with a single neatly folded sweatshirt, and a small display case for travel souvenirs. One whole wall was covered in bookshelves, and the spines weren't all computer related; Akane could make out sci-fi and ghost stories, volumes of mythology, and the darker kind of fairytales.

<144>

But all she could really focus on was that screen Leona had clicked to life and the blazing red words that filled it.

GET OUT.

"I don't understand," she whispered. *John, what's happening? Are you already in trouble? Am I too late?*

"Neither do I," said Leona grimly. "John did not write that."

"How did you see it?"

"Oh, I've been coming into his room and sneaking onto his computer," said Leona with a casual shrug. "I mean, obviously I have, for weeks. I'm amazed I've been getting away with it for so long. But he's not allowed to contact us except once a week by landline, so maybe he couldn't stop me."

"Or didn't want to," said Akane slowly. "Maybe he was leaving a channel open."

"Anyway, he knew I'd try to spy, so I was expecting a message at some point. But that, there? That isn't it."

Akane peered at the screen, frowning. "How do you know?"

"Oh, that's definitely not John. He'd be much ruder." Leona tilted her head. "Is there some way you can check for sure?"

Akane pulled out the chair swiftly and sat down. "It's not John's MO. But it must be coming from his laptop or his phone. He must have set it up to make a copy of what he was doing at the Center, like making notes for later. You know how diligent he is." Akane's eyes widened in realization. "It must have been his phone that sent this. It would have copied whenever he connected to an outside server. And that happened when I messaged him on the sly."

"So why *this*? It's kinda curt."

<145>

Akane bit her lip. "I don't know. It looks like his own phone's been hacked."

"He's in trouble," said Leona.

"I think so. Because this—this *thing*—is not how he works." Akane tapped at the keyboard, then leaned closer and tried again, her fingertips flying. "And I can't shift it. Who's telling him to get out, and why?"

"'John is the computer,' that's what Dad used to say." Leona wrinkled her nose in distaste. "But he is *not* that gruesome font, for a *start*."

This made things worse. In her head, Akane debated for a moment whether to tell Leona the truth about what she'd discovered. But how could she explain it to John's sister before she even tried to tell John? She didn't even know whether the girl could keep a secret.

"I've been worried too," she said at last. "There've been a few . . . odd communications. That's why I'm going to find him."

"What, by sneaking out the utility room window?" Leona grinned. "I've tried that. The security light comes on, and Grandpa's dogs raise a fit. It's better to go out my bedroom window, down onto the lower roof. But—" she sighed. "Even if you made it . . . I don't know about your grandma, but Mom will have the whole Fairbanks police force after you in about five minutes."

Akane's shoulders slumped. "But I have to get to John!" she blurted.

"Sh!" Leona glanced at the door. "I think so too, but there's a better way. My boyfriend, Brody, is a pilot, and he flies to Wales Airport like *all* the time. How about I arrange a girls' trip to the national park out there?" She grinned. "Well, teenagers' trip.

<146>

Then I can get quality time with Brody, and you can go check on John. There'll be some kind of ferry or something going out to the island, I bet."

"Seriously?" Akane's eyes widened. "That would be so much faster too."

"Yup. And meanwhile your grandma can hang out in Fairbanks with my mom for a few days, blissfully unaware and *not calling the cops*."

Akane sprang out of the chair and hugged her. "You are the best big sister."

"I know," sighed Leona, tossing her hair. "Just make sure you tell John when you see him."

<147>

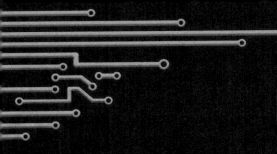

Twenty

Neither Adam nor Leo would meet John's eyes. The
Shark Twins didn't have their usual cocksure, arrogant look;
they were propped against the wall of the basketball court, grim
faced and sulky, ignoring everyone. No wonder, thought John,
after that tongue-lashing from Roy Lykos. Maybe they even felt
guilty about their contagious malware wrecking the entire school
system.

But that didn't mean he couldn't add to their shame. Anger
rising inside him, John scrambled to his feet.

Salome tugged at his arm, alarmed. "Where are you going?
You're in enough trouble for being late."

"I'm going to tell those two what I think of them."

"You go right ahead," said Slack, standing up. "I want to hear
this myself."

Salome grabbed his belt and dragged him back down. "Jake!
Don't you get involved," she snapped. "If John has to get it off his
chest, let him. It doesn't mean you all have to start a fight."

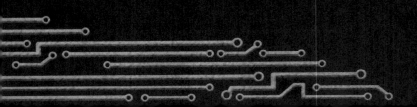

Slack looked like he was about to argue, but he subsided with a scowl. "Yes, Mom."

John clenched his fists and made his way over to the two boys, stepping over his fellow students crowded on the floor. Imogen Black gave him only a fleeting glance before returning to her conversation with Carlos Sanchez Ramirez. Ms. Reiffelt wasn't even in the hall any longer; she'd gone with the other staff members to fight the malware. Nobody would care, thought John, if he scrubbed those two malicious bugs off the system—

Stop that. Shaking himself, he halted in front of Adam and Leo. "What did you do to my phone?"

Adam turned sharply. LED light glinted on his glasses. "What?"

"The hack on my phone. The frozen screen."

"Your phone got hacked before Irma La Douche confiscated it?" Leo grinned suddenly. "Ha ha! That'll teach you to play with the big boys, noob."

"You know it got hacked!" snapped John. *Thank goodness I didn't let on that I still have it; that was close.* "Get it cleaned off as soon as you get your laptops back, or—"

"Or what?" Adam shoved forward, bringing his face close to John's. "You'll tell the teacher?" he mocked in a singsong voice. "You little punk. They're not going to discipline me. I'm Rick Kruz's son, and I belong here more than you ever will."

His breath smelled of pepperoni, and John recoiled in disgust. "Your dad's Rick Kruz. Big deal. That doesn't give you the right to wreck every device in the school!"

<149>

Adam grabbed his collar and yanked him closer. "You've got some nerve. If you hadn't—"

Leo gave his friend a sharp, deliberate kick in the leg. Adam caught his breath and pressed his lips together.

"If I hadn't what?" demanded John.

For a moment there was panic in Adam's eyes. Then his face relaxed into its usual sneer. "If you'd set up a proper firewall, nobody could have hacked your stupid phone. Don't blame us just because *you* were careless."

"So, it was you! I swear I'll—"

"We've got nothing to do with that!" exploded Leo, shoving him away from Adam. "You think we'd waste our time on you? We've got better things to do, Laine. Go fix your own mistakes."

They were both glowering at him now. John's chest heaved with fury, but the teachers were starting to throw glances their way. Salome was right: the last thing he needed was to get into even more trouble, after he'd arrived panting in digital quarantine just as the doors were closing. And he certainly didn't want any awkward questions about what he'd been doing to make him late and what he might have overheard.

Turning on his heels, John stalked away, ignoring the muttered insults from Adam and Leo. *I know they did it. Those vicious—*

He hesitated, staring down at a rare clear patch of floor. *No, you don't,* Parallel John reminded him in the back of his brain. *You don't know they did it.* And they'd been adamant they weren't responsible.

John didn't know Adam and Leo well, and he didn't want to, but he couldn't help thinking that if they'd hacked his phone,

<150>

they'd want him to know it. The pair had gloated openly about hijacking Eva's laptop. Why bother to deny that they'd compromised John's phone?

John felt a quiver of uncertainty. *They wouldn't deny it. They'd laugh in my face.* So why hadn't they?

Into the fog of doubt crept a small, clear moment from that confrontation. *You've got some nerve. If you hadn't—*

And then Leo had kicked Adam, quite sharply.

Adam was definitely the alpha in that twisted friendship, John thought, and he'd never have expected Leo to shut him up.

If I hadn't done—what? The Shark Twins hadn't been talking about John's phone at that point; they'd been talking about the malware that had infected the school. *What did I do?*

John glanced toward Imogen and Carlos. The two teachers were deep in conversation, their backs half turned to him. Making a spur-of-the-moment decision, he headed casually toward the weight room corridor.

It was the outer door of the gym complex that had been locked; the swing doors between the basketball court and the weight room didn't even have a latch. With a last quick glance over his shoulder, John pushed one side ajar and slipped through.

The low hubbub of conversation in the basketball court faded to almost nothing. John's heart beat rapidly as he stared at the empty corridor. *So what now, clever boy?* he wondered sarcastically. There was no way past the outer gym door.

He turned to the plate glass windows of the workout room. The displays on the aerobic equipment were all still frozen on that irritating low-res dinosaur. John let out an exasperated sigh and opened the door.

It smelled of sweat that had been polished with disinfectant wipes, but at least it was completely quiet. Climbing onto one of the stationary cycles, John gave the pedals a desultory push. The screen didn't greet him by name. Instead, the velociraptor grinned at him obstinately.

John pressed his finger hard on the display. *If you hadn't*—If I hadn't what?

And with a suddenness that shocked the breath from his lungs, the dinosaur vanished. Letters formed in the emptiness.

John Laine is on the stationary cycle. Hello John Laine!

How in the actual—he thought, blinking. Is the bug fixed already?

The letters dissolved and reformed. **John Laine is on the computer.**

No, I'm not, you stupid machine. That isn't how this works. Frowning, John prodded the screen again, hard enough to leave a faded impression of his forefinger. But the screen wouldn't cooperate.

John is on the computer.

John gritted his teeth. "I'm in the gym," he told it out loud. "That bug really got to you, huh?"

John is on the computer.

He gave a growl of annoyance. "Suit yourself." There was no reason for a cursor to appear; there wasn't a keypad. A touch of the fingerprint was how this thing operated. So why had one suddenly blinked into life, flickering between the letters?

The cursor blinked and jumped back, deleting a word.

John is the computer.

He froze.

<152>

John is the computer.

His throat was so tight that he could only whisper it. *"Dad?"*

No. Dad's dead. The room spun around him. Could it be Roy Lykos? Some bizarre test, maybe—or was Roy trying to help John? If they'd met at some medical conference, his dad could have mentioned that family phrase to Roy, told him about it for amusement. Roy might have remembered.

No. Why would he remember a passing conversation with a man he hardly knew? Why would Dad even tell him? Short of breath, John slammed the screen with his forefinger, over and over again. *What kind of malware taunts you with a family joke?*

At last the words dissolved, and he panted with relief. Something sparked on the display again, and this time it flashed so brightly it looked *enraged.*

DO YOU KNOW HOW CLOSE YOU CAME?

John flinched back so fast, he almost tumbled off the bike. The meaning of the words clicked instantly in his head. They linked so smoothly with a recent memory that he could hear Roy's angry voice as he berated Adam and Leo. *Do you know how close he came?*

He'd been focused on Roy's infuriated bark: *That's what triggered this shutdown!* The man's previous words hadn't registered at the time. But there they were now, right in front of him in Helvetica Bold.

DO YOU KNOW HOW CLOSE YOU CAME?

It was me, John thought as a chill rippled up and down his spine. *It was something I did.* But what, and when? He'd only wanted to clean that malware off of Eva's computer. It was all he'd focused on for days—weeks, almost. And he'd come

<153>

nowhere near succeeding, until that moment *on another planet* when all the Parallel Johns had gotten busy in his head . . .

DO YOU KNOW HOW CLOSE YOU CAME?

The screen was changing yet again. Shooting a nervous glance at the other aerobic equipment, John could make out only that maddening dinosaur—but this solitary display, on this bike alone, was dissolving into an image. The shape of a boy, shattering into pixels. It reformed and disintegrated again.

John's heart was beating so hard he thought it might break his ribcage. He could only watch, dizzy and sick, as the vision from his own private dreams was played out over and over on the screen in front of him.

He squeezed his eyes shut and opened them again. The image was still there, replaying at four-second intervals: the boy who died in a blizzard of pixels. Was it a boy? He wasn't sure anymore. He leaned close to the screen, shading it desperately with his cupped hands. It might be a girl.

It was a girl. It was Eva Vygotsky.

<154>

Twenty-One

John didn't know how long he sat there, immobile.
He didn't want to kill Eva. He hadn't killed her. He *wouldn't* kill her. *How did this machine know about his nightmares?*

John swung off the bike; his thoughts were a turmoil of indecision. As he stood clenching and unclenching his fists, the glass door of the gym flung open. Salome and Slack stared at him.

"What are you *doing?*" demanded Salome in a strained whisper. "You're supposed to be in the court!"

"You sure pick the wrong time for a workout," said Slack. "Come on, you're going to get us all in trouble."

"I can't go back in there." John's heart thrashed in his chest. "I think someone at this school has it in for me. The machines sure do."

"What?" demanded Salome. "Are you crazy?"

"Don't be nuts," scoffed Slack. "This isn't *Terminator.*"

Frustrated and bewildered, John clutched his head. "Not the machines, of course—but someone's sending me messages through them."

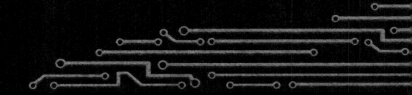

"They're sending *everyone* a message." Salome pointed at the velociraptor displays.

"And the message," said Slack with a smirk, "is that Adam and Leo are jerks."

"Quiet, Jake," snapped Salome, and Slack was instantly quiet. "John, calm down. What are you talking about?"

He took deep breaths and shut his eyes as he wondered how to explain. "The messages I'm getting are *different*. It's not the malware. They're trying to scare me, or—or warn me. I'm not sure which. I think maybe Roy hacked my phone and those machines. He *could*. He'd know how." John blinked his eyes open. "And if it's him, he's warning me about something."

"Warning you about what?" Salome raised her eyebrows disapprovingly. "I see you've managed to keep your phone, John. Give it to me."

"It's useless, anyway. I can't operate it at all." Meekly, he took it from his pocket and handed it over; she took it and frowned. John turned to Slack. "You know I told you about that conversation I overheard? Between Yasuo and Ms. Reiffelt? They were arguing—really fighting. About *flies* that they'd caught. Someone they had in their *possession*."

"Odd . . . " murmured Salome. "But you know the Center works with a lot of corporations . . . "

"It wasn't about some commercial research project; I know it. It sounded more sinister, and they were talking about *people*. About something that started *the day the two of us arrived*."

"Pfft. What would be special about us?" But Slack scratched at the palm of his left hand and looked suddenly nervous.

<156>

"Slack—we were the only students who *did* arrive that day. Ms. Reiffelt is up to something bad, and it's something to do with us, and Yasuo's involved."

"Yasuo *Yamamoto*?" Salome almost dropped the phone.

"Is there another Yasuo?" snapped John. "And there's this hidden room at the bottom of the school, Lab 31. Roy was investigating it; I followed him—oh, I know it sounds crazy, and I don't have any proof. You'll have to take my word for it. And I've been having these nightmares, and—"

"Nightmares?" Slack started. "Me too."

"You have?" John gaped at him. "You haven't said—it didn't show—"

Slack shrugged. "I'm a really sound sleeper. I just wake up, and they're gone. But they make me so angry."

"Look, I swear I'm not panicking over nothing." John took a breath, forcing himself to be calm and deadly serious. "There's something strange going on here. Something wrong."

Salome stared at him for a few long seconds. "You're serious." It wasn't a question.

"I am. I don't know for sure that the messages are from Roy. But someone here is up to something bad, and whoever they are, they think I'm a threat." John's throat tightened. "The trouble is," he whispered, "I think they might be right."

"You," said Slack. "A threat? You're having bad dreams is all, and—"

"It's not just the nightmares." John looked up miserably into Slack's eyes. "I'm getting the same feelings during the day. I keep wanting to kill them. Adam and Leo, I mean. I can hardly hold

<157>

myself back. And I'm scared. I'm scared one day I'm going to do it."

"You're thirteen years old," said Salome. There was a fearful undercurrent in her voice. "How could you kill anybody? Don't be silly."

John bristled. "I'm not being *silly*. I'm honestly worried. I think—Salome, I think there's something wrong, for sure. But it's something wrong with *me*."

Slack was very silent, staring at the floor. "If there's something wrong with you," he said, clearing his throat, "there's something wrong with me too."

"What?"

"I get the same thing. I mean, the nightmares are like wish fulfillment. I *love* them. Why do you think I've been spending so much time in the gym? I need to work out the rage."

"You didn't say anything!"

"No, and I didn't say anything about the nightmares either," snapped Slack. "And neither did you. Because it sounds *ridiculous*."

"Somebody's sending me messages," said John. "Somebody who can bypass the worst malware I've ever seen, one the teachers can't even fix. Maybe it's Roy; maybe it's the same person who installed the bug. It's telling me to get out. I don't know if that's because this person hates me or because they want to help me. I don't *know*."

Salome was looking from John to Slack and back again. Her expression was unreadable. She was so quiet, for so long, that at last they turned to stare at her.

<158>

Her expression made the back of John's neck prickle. "I've had the nightmares too," she said, her voice barely more than a whisper. "The same ones. I've dreamed about killing Adam and Leo, and it feels real, and it's terrifying, but it's not *gory* real, it's like—"

"Like you're just deleting them," said John quietly.

They stared at one another. Salome's jaw tightened. Her eyes once again held a cool, rational light.

"It's a strange coincidence," she said at last. "And I don't believe in coincidences. I take it none of us started having these dreams till we came here, right?" She glanced questioningly at them and nodded. "So it's something in this Center."

"But we can't just leave," objected Slack.

"Indeed." Salome made a face.

John gulped. "And if we're imagining the whole thing—which I don't think we are—"

Salome said, "We're not imagining it."

"What?" The two boys spoke together.

Salome held out John's phone. "There's another message," she whispered.

John snatched it from her hand. He stared at the screen, frozen in shock.

The flashing words were gone, and a fuzzy black-and-white image had formed. For a crazy moment he thought the device was streaming a movie: the silhouettes of two black helicopters were flying low toward him across a snow-covered ocean.

The flies are already caught.

Why did Ms. Reiffelt's overheard words suddenly trigger a hideous premonition in his brain?

<159>

Six weeks and five days. The flies are caught.

John shuddered as he took a breath. There were letters and numbers in the bottom corner of the screen, ticking in some sort of countdown.

"Is this *real?*"

"It looks real," said Salome. "It looks like security cam footage."

"But they look like military," said Slack. He looked utterly confused.

"They are." Salome took the phone back. "And it's live. Look at the time stamp."

"But that can't be anything to do with *us!*"

"Who knows?" Salome thrust the phone back into John's hand. "But it's one more weird coincidence, and it's *not good.*"

"We need help," said John desperately.

"But whom can we ask?" said Slack. "Not Ms. Reiffelt, that's for sure. McAuliffe? Ramirez? Imogen Black?"

"No." Salome shook her head. "We barely know them!"

"I trust Roy. But I don't know where he is," said John with rising fear. "He's not on the basketball court. He's probably in the east wing at the mainframe by now."

"And that is a problem how?" snapped Salome, as she indicated the room around them. "We're not in the basketball court either."

"The door's locked!" said John impatiently.

"But it's not electronically locked," said Salome. "They can't use any computerized devices, remember? They locked it with an actual key. And if you think I don't know how to pick a lock . . . "

"Uh," said Slack, his eyes boggling. "That's *exactly* what I think."

<160>

"Then you'd be wrong."

John gave her a startled look. Prissy, too-good-to-be-true Salome? She could pick a *lock*?

He shook himself. There wasn't time to ask. "If we really can get out and contact him, Roy's going to know what to do. And even if he thinks we're being ridiculous, he won't laugh at us; he'll explain *why* we're being ridiculous."

"Which we probably are." Slack's expression was filled with desperate hope.

"Then let's go and make fools of ourselves," said Salome, "before we change our minds."

<161>

Twenty-Two

"Your feet are too loud." Salome turned around glaring at Slack.

"I'm *trying*." He returned her glower.

"Let's just stay in the shadows," said John nervously.

The atrium was deserted and so were the corridors leading from it. There was no one to see them as they crept from the gym complex, but instinctively and without even discussing it, they'd all slunk close to the wall as they made their way toward the east wing.

"It's going to be fine," whispered Salome, as if she were talking to herself. "Nearly there, nearly there . . . "

The passage that led to the mainframe was ahead, just beyond the pool corridor; it was filled with darkness like all the others. Maybe, thought John, the technical staff wasn't even there. Maybe *Roy* wasn't there.

But they had to be at the mainframe. Where else would they go when malware had infected the Center? John paused, his back to the wall, his heart pounding.

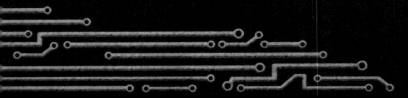

We're being crazy. We're imagining the whole thing. Why do I feel so scared?

But those helicopters . . .

As they passed the pool corridor, Salome halted abruptly and darted into its entrance. She didn't say a word, but she clutched John's arm tightly enough to hurt. He got the message. He turned quickly to Slack behind him.

Quiet, he mouthed and pulled his friend back into the shadowed corridor. The smell of chlorine stung his nostrils.

Salome was pointing around the corner as her finger shook. Her breathing was silent, but John could see her chest rising and falling rapidly. He and Slack peered past her.

Roy Lykos stood at the darkened entrance to the mainframe corridor. And beside him stood a man dressed entirely in black.

Not fashionable black, like Roy himself. *Military* black, with boots and a Kevlar vest and a balaclava. Even his eyes were in shadow. And none of that was as unnerving as the gun he cradled in his arms.

John didn't dare to voice aloud the questions he was desperate to ask. *Is Roy in trouble? What does this guy want?*

Why is his gun lowered?

And why does Roy look so calm?

In the echoing emptiness, Roy's murmuring voice carried clearly.

"I'll bring them from the gym complex. They're there now, and they're not going anywhere."

The gunman nodded once. *He's not threatening Roy*, thought John, his lungs contracting painfully. *He's taking orders.*

<163>

"Let me be clear: I want those kids secured. Once I turn them over to you, they're not to be out of your custody at any point. They're not to be out of your *sight*."

The gunman spoke at last, hoarse and throaty. "What about the Vygotsky girl?"

"I'll deal with the faulty one later. The functioning subjects are the top priority." Light gleamed on Roy Lykos's eyes, and they were steely and cold. "I need those three out of this Center and under my sole control. No mistakes, do you understand?"

"If there's trouble, Mr. Freki?"

"Restrain the children as necessary. But do not harm them—do I make myself clear? These are valuable properties, and the firearms are for persuasion only. Do your men understand that?"

"If they don't, I'll shoot them first," rasped the gunman. He didn't sound menacing. He sounded like he was confirming a bank request. "But my men do understand. Perfectly."

"Then wait here. I'll bring the subjects. There are staff members present, several of whom are unaware of this project and entirely innocent. I don't anticipate trouble, but they may follow me, and they may protest." For a moment, Roy paused. "Them, you can shoot."

The gunman withdrew into the shadows of the mainframe corridor. John couldn't even move. *I didn't hear any of that. I'm dreaming. Who is Mr. Freki? That's Roy Lykos! This is insane. Wake up. Wake up.*

A hand gripped his arm, and he almost yelped. "Salome," he breathed, his heart thundering.

Her trembling voice was barely audible. "We need to get out of here. We really do."

<164>

"We didn't imagine it." Slack even *sounded* pale.

"There's nowhere to go." John could hear his voice rising in panic, and he was powerless to stop it. *Roy Lykos? Roy is a bad guy? I don't understand . . .*

"We have to try," hissed Slack. "Get out through the roof? Steal a boat?"

"We won't make it!" Salome's eyes were white rimmed with fear.

No, four people were never going to make it out of a cyber-complex past heavily armed gunmen and the digital genius that was Roy Lykos. John's heart felt as if it would burst with fear—

Wait. Four people? He turned slowly and stared into black-rimmed eyes. Eva stood behind them, silent and icy calm, her lips a pale straight line.

"You will make it out." She was quiet and intense. "I will take you."

"*How?*" Salome clenched her fists, paralyzed by indecision. "Where did you—why would you believe us? I'm not sure *I* believe—"

"You're my friends. You're in trouble." Eva glanced at John. "Helping is what you do, yes? You are running out of time. So come with me."

She was so calm, so rational, while John's brain spun out of control and Salome and Slack looked like malfunctioning autom-atons. *What happened back there? Why did Eva come to find us?*

The faulty one. How can she be "faulty"? Eva was a serene picture of sanity in the madness that had suddenly enveloped them. There wasn't a flicker of panic on her face as she turned to lead them into the total darkness of the pool corridor.

Yet why could John feel her fear like a tangible, prickling force?

<165>

Twenty-Three

"I know the ways in and out of this place," Eva assured them, as they crowded frantically into a cleaning cupboard next to the changing rooms. "I don't like being confined in this Center, and I like it *even less* when people always know where I am."

She closed the door silently behind them, and they stood for a moment in darkness till she clicked on a tiny key fob flashlight. Slack and Salome's faces looked ghostly and scared in the thin white glow, and John realized he must look much the same.

"Where to now?" His voice was still quivering with shock. "We can't hide in here forever."

Eva held up a finger to silence him, then dragged a set of folding steps from behind a vacuum cleaner. Snapping them open, she positioned them in the middle of the cupboard, grabbed a mop, and climbed up. She raised the mop and gave a single jab at the ceiling.

A hatch gave way, flopping open with a clatter that made them jump.

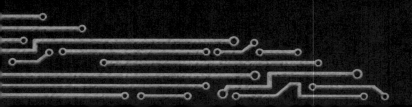

"There." Eva pointed into the darkness above them and handed the little flashlight to Salome. "Heating vents. I'll show you." She jumped, grabbed the edge of the hatch, and hauled herself up. Her black boots dangled for a moment, then vanished.

I have to get a grip, John realized. *I don't know what's happening or what Lykos is up to, but we need to get out of here. It's all that matters right now.*

Taking a deep breath, John climbed the two steps, jumped for a handhold, and pulled himself up. Inside the tunnel there was total blackness, but when his eyes adjusted, he could make out the pale glow of Eva's hair.

John scooted along the passage on his hands and knees toward her. Behind him he heard a grunt from Slack as he followed. Finally, Salome climbed up, silent and graceful, the little flashlight gripped between her teeth. She too seemed to have calmed down, and there was a glint of determination in her dark eyes.

"Where to now?" she mumbled through the flashlight, then took it from her mouth and stretched past the boys to hand it back to Eva.

"Follow," said Eva, turning to crawl along the vent.

Despite the cramped conditions, the Russian girl was as quiet as a cat, and John felt clumsy and far too noisy as he tried to hurry after her. His hands and boots clanged dully on the metal surface, and Eva turned to throw him an exasperated glare, but behind him Slack sounded even more awkward.

Despite the frequent gym visits, Slack was panting, and as the passage narrowed, he gave a grunt of frustration.

"It's hot in here."

<167>

"It's going to get hotter," came Eva's voice from ahead. "There's a turn ahead, and then there's a vertical shaft, so be careful."

"It can't be too high a climb from this level?" whispered John.

"It's not a climb; it's a descent. We're going to the bottom of the island." Once again, Eva's eyes gleamed as she turned her head. "Those helicopters—they'll have headed for the school's helipad, right? At least one of them will be landing. It would be pretty stupid to go there."

Fair enough, thought John. "How do you know about the helicopters?"

"I saw them coming. I was outside ten minutes ago. I told you: I do not like being trapped."

Of course. She disappeared before everyone was locked in the gym.

The tunnel narrowed again at the corner, and John felt his shoulders brush against the sides. Eva, small and slight, had squirmed around as easily as a snake in a hole. John wriggled and forced his head through, but his shoulder scraped painfully against the metal to his left, and panic rose in his gut. He wriggled a hand free and tried to push himself forward, but he was jammed tight.

"I'm stuck. Eva, I'm stuck!" His whisper was high and hoarse.

She flicked her hair out of her face and twisted to look back. He could have sworn she rolled her eyes.

"Grab my ankles." Eva shuffled backward. "Relax your shoulders."

Flailing with his one free hand, he seized her thin ankle just above her boot, and she crawled forward awkwardly. *She's so small, and she's not strong,* he realized with a lurch of fear as his body became stuck again and jerked.

<168>

Then she gave a grunt and a heave and yanked him forward, his shoulders slipping through, his T-shirt sleeve catching on a metal seam. Stifling a yelp of pain, John dragged himself free on his elbows and kicked his legs wildly to get them around the corner. Then he flopped, panting.

"Get Slack," said Eva calmly.

John twisted his head. Slack's face was behind him, the whites of his goggling eyes shining in the darkness.

"Grab my ankles, Slack . . . "

Slack's shoulders were even broader than John's, and it took a mighty heave to get him around the angle of the vent, but at last he tumbled through, landing with a resounding boom on the metal floor.

"Shh!" came a harsh whisper from behind. "And get out of the way, Jake!"

Slack scuffled forward a few inches on his belly. "Grab my ankles, Salo—"

Salome appeared, twisting herself lithely and easily around the bend. "What was the holdup? You made a huge racket."

John couldn't help grinning with relief. *Trust Salome to do it with elegance.*

"The vertical shaft is wider, so it'll be easier," murmured Eva. "Careful, though. It's just a few feet ahead of me."

She paused and dived forward, and her head and shoulders vanished. John heard a light bump, and Eva's face reappeared, ghostly white and smiling. "There's enough room in the shaft to twist so you can land on your feet. After that, it's easy," she told him.

"Are there steps? Rungs?"

<169>

"No. But the sections are crudely welded. Just grip the seams. They run horizontally, every two feet or so." Eva retreated, disappearing smoothly into the vertical vent.

John took a few deep breaths and gave himself a moment's delay by turning his head to relay the instructions to Slack. There was a nagging, shooting pain in his shoulder: *I tore the skin along with my T-shirt,* he realized.

He was sweating so much, John was worried he would simply shoot down the vertical shaft like a greased eel. He could feel an updraft of cool air on his face, and there was an echoey quality to the sound of Eva's light movements that told him it was indeed a broader tunnel.

But vertical, though . . .

John sucked in a breath and lunged forward.

His damp hand slipped on the metal, and for a horrible moment he felt as if he were hovering over infinity. Then he grasped the edge tighter and flipped his head down as he'd seen Eva do.

His body swung, and his feet followed the rest of him, skittering down the side of the shaft. For a moment his fingers gripped the edge for dear life as his legs dangled loose. Then he found a welded seam with his toes, and he paused, upright at last, his head swimming with relief.

And then he began to climb down.

He couldn't even watch Slack perform the awkward maneuver above him; he was too focused on finding toe- and handholds for himself—and anyway, if Slack fell, he and Eva were both going down with him. *Why worry?* he told himself with a slightly hysterical giggle.

<170>

The shaft seemed endless. Every time he found a grip on the slick sides, he felt that he'd never be able to move to the next hand- or foothold. *I'll just stay here.* But then every time, he forced himself to reach for another ridge of hard solder. He was glad he couldn't see the bottom of this black shaft. Because if he could—

I'd fall.

And that was a bad thought. It was so bad it had frozen him to where he clung. His head reeling, he pressed himself against the side of the vent and panted.

Eva's voice rose up from far below. "Move! John!"

"I can't."

"You have to," came Slack's voice from above him. "John. *John.* Are you scared of *heights?*"

Yes, he thought. Yes, it turns out I am. *And this is a fine time to find out.* How on earth had he coped with the climbing wall?

Because your brain knew it wasn't real, an inner voice told him. *This is.*

"It's real," he murmured faintly.

"Well," Eva's voice floated up. "You have to move anyway."

There was something about her cool, emotionless voice that cut through the panic. John breathed hard, trying to slow his heartbeat. With trembling fingers, he felt along the welded seam for a thicker lump of solder, then lowered one foot to the next ridge.

"Good man," whispered Slack above him.

After that, John shut his eyes and climbed down by his sense of touch alone. It was easier. *And if I fall, I'm not opening my eyes. I'll just keep them shut till I hit the—*

Ground.

<171>

The sole of his foot rested on solid, level steel. "You made it," said Eva. He couldn't see her smile of approval, but he could hear it.

John slumped against the bottom of the shaft, panting, as Slack and Salome scuttled down behind him.

"That was higher than I expected," said Salome.

Her words held an edge of relief: she sounded nearly as scared as he was, and John felt a twinge of validation.

"We're practically at sea level now," said Eva. "Not much farther. And this is a maintenance tunnel, so it's wider. You have to crouch but not crawl."

Slack stiffened abruptly. "Did anyone hear that?"

They all froze, but John raised his head, staring up at the vent they'd just descended.

It was distant but clear. A rhythmic thump on metal, confident and fast and growing louder.

"They're coming after us!" Salome's voice was high with panic.

"Not very fast," said Eva calmly. "Every one of them is bigger than we are."

Slack turned to stare down the tunnel. "They could cut us off at the other end—"

"Then I suggest," said Eva, "that we move quickly."

They made faster progress in the maintenance tunnel, driven by their urgent terror. Bent over double, the four of them could almost jog, the flashlight bouncing feebly ahead of them in Eva's fist. John focused on putting one foot in front of the other, his head low and intent, and it was only an odd, echoing crash and boom that brought him up short.

"What's that?" he hissed. "The gunmen?"

<172>

Eva stopped. She switched off the flashlight, but they weren't plunged into darkness; a shimmering, greenish light gleamed on her pale hair. There was a cool breeze that wasn't air-conditioning, and into John's nostrils crept a salty, ozone tang.

"No." Eva smiled. "It's the sea."

<173>

Twenty-Four

Eva yanked back a lever on the barred gate at the tunnel's end. As she swung it open, they stepped out onto wet rock lashed by spray. Beside John, Salome inhaled the cold air with a gasp of delight. The next moment, a violent shudder ran through her body.

"I forgot it was winter!" she wailed.

Out toward the horizon, there was a smear of iron gray that lay between the sky and the sea, and wet flakes of snow were already drifting down to pockmark the water's surface closer to shore. John felt faint with relief: there were no dark figures waiting for them. But the jagged rocks to the right and left were edged with white, and as John, Slack, and Salome stepped beyond the cave mouth, a biting wind knocked them back.

"That blizzard's going to be on us in minutes," Slack yelled against the roar of the waves. "We can't survive out here."

"Yes, you can." Eva was rummaging in a gap between boulders within the cave. With an effort, she dragged out a huge zippered bag. "Winter clothes," she explained, opening it as they clustered

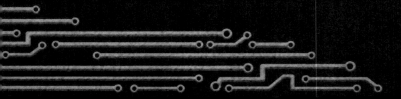

around her, rubbing their arms. "You think I go exploring in my shirtsleeves?"

"How many jackets do you need?" Slack was raking through the clothes in wonder.

"I've been collecting them." Eva shrugged. "For a snowy day."

"You've been stealing them," said Salome in shock. "Chima said he'd had to ask his parents to send a new coat—"

"I've been liberating them," said Eva firmly. "Chima's parents can afford it. And so can the others."

Salome opened her mouth to protest again, but John put a hand on her arm. It wasn't as if they could spare any moral indignation right now. Salome glanced at him and shut up.

Rapidly, Eva shared the contents of the bag: insulated jackets, waterproof pants, beanie hats, and thermal gloves. "Your own boots will have to do," she remarked, peering at their feet. "They're not bad. I mean, at least Salome isn't wearing her Converse. And I hope we don't have to go far for now."

"Where *are* we going?" asked Slack, yanking a pair of thick waterproof pants over his jeans.

"The only place we can go," pointed out Eva. "Diomede City."

If Leona had heard her call it a city, thought John, his sister would have a fit. He could see most of it by now, that cluster of scattered low houses he remembered from the helicopter flight—but although it wasn't far away, it was taking them too long to get there. The snowstorm had made landfall now. Driven from the north by the fierce gale, it blustered against their backs and soaked their hairlines; cold flakes melted on John's neck and

<175>

dribbled down his spine. At least the wind wasn't in their faces, but it shoved them forward, making them stumble as they picked their way around the wave-lashed coastline. And at any moment he expected a hunting party to round the next bend, bounding toward them.

Another breaker smashed onto the rocks beside him, soaking his jacket and foaming around his feet. John pulled his hood tighter over his head and paused to catch Salome's arm before she could slip and fall.

"Eva, what do we do when we get there?" he yelled.

She turned, squinting into the wind. Despite Eva's small stature, John and the others had struggled to keep up with her. She hopped and scampered over the rocks like a pro.

"We hide," she shouted and ran on.

John rubbed wet snow from his face and plowed grimly onward. The helicopters' occupants were in the Wolf's Den by now, hunting them, but where had the aircraft gone? John couldn't hear engines or rotors. Was there space on the school's heliport for two craft? Where else would the other one have gone?

Eva was running over loose rocks, and John picked up speed, dodging the waves. Behind him he could hear the pounding, splashing steps of Slack and Salome. The cold air burning his aching lungs, he raced after the Russian girl as she dived into the cover of a big warehouse.

Panting, all four of them slumped against the wall. "What now?" gasped Salome.

Thoughtfully, Eva peered around the corner and pointed one gloved hand. Slack sucked in a breath and cursed.

<176>

The broad strip of land that extended out from the village was blurred by snowfall, but the monstrous silhouette out there was distinct enough.

"One of the helicopters landed on the Diomede City helipad," explained Eva, unnecessarily.

"But that means they'll have men in the village," said Salome bleakly.

"And it won't take them long to find us," pointed out John. "It's not exactly Anchorage. We've got minutes, if we're lucky."

"We may not even have that." Salome sounded grim, as she lifted her right hand, palm forward.

"Oh no," groaned Slack. "The implants."

John gave a snarl of frustration and hammered his palm against the wall of the warehouse. "If my phone was working, we could try to disable them. But it *isn't*."

"And breaking your hand won't help." Salome firmly took it and forced it back to his side.

"I know hiding places on the island," said Eva, "but it's a small island. Even without the implants, we couldn't evade them for long."

And that was when John's phone buzzed.

The four of them stared at it and then at each other.

"I thought you said it wasn't working?" said Slack.

"It wasn't! I—" John stared at the screen.

You have to get off the island.

John froze. *What the—*

John it's me. Akane. I can't explain.

He prodded the keypad furiously.

Phone was broken! Terminally! How'd you hack? How'd you fix—

<177>

NOT NOW. John! Get off the island. I will meet you. Somehow. On the mainland. You need to leave the ISLAND.

How do I know it's you?

There was screen silence. John clenched his jaw so hard it hurt. *Those creeps. Lykos pretended to be a father to me, and now he's pretending to be my best friend. He's tricking me. I don't know how, but—*

Sound rippled out of the phone, the fluid song of a Japanese bush warbler. And simultaneously an image blossomed on the screen: an eye, dark rimmed, its iris a blinding white.

White Eye!

It's Akane.

It really is.

She'd hacked him to help him, just as he'd done for her before that thwarted BASE jump . . .

John, there's no time to explain. They're after you. GET TO WALES.

"John, what's the message?" demanded Salome.

His teeth still gritted, John met her eyes, cold and calm. "We have to get off the island."

Salome and Slack stared at each other and at Eva, who nodded calmly.

"I'm not kidding," growled John. "Now! We're running out of time!"

"Who *was* that?" Slack glared suspiciously at the resurrected phone.

John bit back his frustration. "Akane, my friend Akane. She says we need to leave the island. She said to go to Wales, and I

<178>

guess she means the airport on the mainland. Those gunmen, they *will find us* if we stay here. You *know* they will!"

Slack glanced anxiously at Salome. "Lykos wants us in his possession—he said so."

"I agree," said Salome grimly. "I'd trust this friend of John's sooner than I'd trust Lykos or his gunmen. So we leave. Now."

Eva nodded at the helicopter on the end of the strip. "That's the only way out. Which is a problem."

"No," said Salome. "It isn't."

"Huh?" John blinked in surprise.

"Don't be crazy," scoffed Slack. "Who's going to fly it for us?"

"I am." Salome pulled her hood back and smiled coolly.

Slack exploded. "*You?*"

"I can fly that thing." Salome stared at the helicopter. "Don't ask."

"Yes, do not ask," said Eva, "because there isn't time. Go."

"Wait, *what?*" Slack's jaw fell open.

John rose to his feet. His resolve was strengthening by the second; besides, did they have any choice? "She said don't ask. C'mon. She can fly."

"What—?"

"I'm not coming," said Eva, taking a step back.

"*What?*" Slack's vocabulary seemed to have shrunk to one word.

"No way!" exclaimed John, seizing Eva's hand.

"I can do this, Eva," said Salome, her voice strangely calm. "You don't need to worry."

"No, it's not that." Gently, Eva dislodged John's grip. "You need someone to stay here. Ground crew. It has to be me. I can monitor you, and them, and misdirect if necessary."

<179>

"But Lykos has it in for you," pleaded John. This was no time to spare either the girl's feelings or her nerves. "He calls you 'the faulty one.' You're not safe, Eva!"

"Listen to me, John Laine." She gazed at him intently. "These people, they are not after me, for now. I am safe, so I will stay. *For now.* You are not safe, so go!"

"Thank you, Eva." For once, Salome seemed oddly disinclined to argue. She gave Eva a quick hug, then ran.

"This is crazy," said John, gripping Eva's hands. "How can you hide?"

"I won't have to. And if I do, I know the places."

Bewildered, John watched Salome bolt for the shoreline and the helipad. *She's so fond of Eva, but she isn't even arguing. I don't understand—* He turned back to Eva, tormented. "We can't leave you! I—"

Eva rolled her eyes. "What is it with you males? I'm not coming. That's *it.* I said *go!*" He gaped at her.

"*Now!*"

There was nothing he could do. John grabbed Slack and yanked him into a run. Wet snow half blinded him, and the wind hit him so hard it almost toppled him, but he recovered his footing and pounded out onto the strip.

Far behind, he thought he heard a yell, but he didn't look back. He kept running grimly, with Slack panting at his side.

As the strip broadened, John felt his feet strike solid concrete. The helicopter loomed ahead. Salome was crouched at its hatch, jabbing at a control panel, and as the boys reached her, the door swung open. Salome vaulted up easily and vanished into the aircraft's belly.

<180>

John jumped onto the landing skid, grabbed the rim of the fuselage, and dragged himself up. Seizing Slack's armpit, he pulled him up and slammed the door shut.

Salome was already in the cockpit, and the two boys jostled into the seats behind her. She was focused on the controls while she flicked switches and peered at dials on the console. She said nothing, and she didn't even glance at Slack and John; there was a cold intensity in her eyes that was unnerving.

The helicopter gave a deafening rattle and roar as Salome seized and opened the throttle, and she clasped the stick to her left and raised it. As the pitch of the engine rose to a whine, she clenched her jaw and pressed the left pedal. John and Slack watched, stunned. Already the craft felt lighter beneath them, and it was swaying slightly.

Salome's left hand and foot worked in perfect synchronicity, gently easing the helicopter up into the wind. It was swaying more wildly now, and she bared her teeth as she balanced it, glancing up toward the rotors. The craft's nose swung left and right, and Salome steadied it.

"Oh my God," whimpered Slack. "We're airborne."

Salome said nothing. She concentrated on the pedal and the throttle, pressing, adjusting, easing, as they rose higher. The helicopter gave a violent lurch and jolt, and she muttered under her breath. John shut his eyes. He was certain now that he heard shouting. And he was even more certain that he'd just heard shots.

Salome ignored it all. She lifted the throttle, depressed the pedal.

Then they rose sharply and smoothly into the wind-tossed sky.

<181>

Twenty-Five

"Bad news," said Salome calmly.

John at last dared to pry open his eyes. At his side, Slack didn't. He was clutching his seatbelt as if that would make it more secure and mumbling what sounded like a fervent prayer.

John unsnapped his seatbelt and moved forward. *If I don't look down, I'll be fine.* "What?"

"We've got company," said Salome.

"You sound like a bad action movie." Slack nervously giggled.

Salome took no notice, and she didn't react as John peered over her shoulder. His stomach lurched, and not only at the glimpse of the heaving gray sea far below. Out of the snow clouds ahead of them, three more sinister black craft were approaching.

"What are those?" he asked with trepidation.

Salome gave him a quick look and returned to the controls.

The three new helicopters were growing bigger by the second, and sweat beads formed on Salome's brow. She reached for the control stick between her knees and veered the craft eastward. Through the murky sky, a coastline emerged.

"Is that Alaska?" Slack had finally opened his eyes and was craning to look out of the window. "The mainland?"

"No," said Salome. "It's Russia. I think those new helicopters are Russian."

"We don't want to go to Russia," said Slack.

"State the obvious, why don't you."

John leaned over to cup his hands to the window. The Russian aircraft loomed large now, bypassing them by several yards, as John cracked a window. The cold air hit him like a vicious slap, but he blinked and peered harder. The Russian helicopters turned elegantly and hung at their rear. Two moved out to flank them; the other swooped alarmingly close to their tail.

"Are they . . . are they *shepherding* us?" asked Slack.

"Yes, but not in a nice way," said Salome. She accelerated, and the Russian helicopters increased their pace, drawing closer. As she made a hesitant turn, one of them flew gracefully to her right, blocking her. Both the flanking helicopters rose and pulled closer together. John stared up at them.

They lowered, tightening Salome's room for maneuvering even further.

"They'll drive us into the water!" yelled John. "Where do they want us to *go?*"

"Russia, *clearly,*" Salome snapped. "I'm trying to dodge them, but they're driving me exactly where they want." She jerked on the control stick, and the craft lurched violently to the left, but the helicopter on that side loomed ominously closer. The pilot waved in a clear gesture of command.

Salome steadied the craft, flying on in the only possible direction. "The gulag it is."

<183>

"Can you increase our altitude?" yelled John desperately. He could make out the faces of the pilots now, their eyes concealed by mirrored sunglasses. They did not look friendly.

"Not in this weather. I could lower the chopper, but we could hit the sea. That would be bad." Nevertheless, she pulled on the left control, and the nose dipped hard toward the water.

"No!" yelled Slack, his voice high and filled with panic. "Up!"

The whole craft shuddered and swayed as Salome fought to lift it. "They've got us where they want us," she shouted over the engine's rattle and roar. "And look!" She took her hand briefly off the cyclic control to point up to her right. "The other chopper's followed us from Diomede. They're close!"

John gasped. The Diomede helicopter was flying fast above the others, angling around to cut them off.

The radio on the control panel crackled to life, and Salome glared at it. John didn't understand the barked words. "What are they saying?"

"My Russian's not brilliant," muttered Salome, "but they're not talking to us. They're warning off the Diomede chopper."

The clashing voices on the radio were rising in volume, and John could make out a few words from the American side. "*Back off . . . return to your base . . . please withdraw immediately . . .*"

"This is going to turn into an international incident!" shrieked Slack grimly.

And suddenly a high female voice joined the others, speaking swift and fluent Russian. Salome was startled.

"What's that?" asked John. His heart was in overdrive.

"It's Eva! Sh!" Salome listened. "She's hacked their radios. She's telling the Russians to focus on protecting us. To back off and

<184>

block the Americans and to give us a clear run to the Siberian border."

Salome's Russian seemed to be *fairly* brilliant, thought John.

The Russian craft swooped high above them and turned. John could just make out all four now, facing each other down, with the Russians barring the Americans' way. The radio argument grew even more heated.

"The Russians won't fall for that for long," he warned.

"Nope." Salome was pulling at the cyclic control again, swinging back toward the Russian coastline, dipping the nose, and accelerating.

"What—" said Slack. "Salome, *where are you going?*"

"That cloudbank." She pointed. "I want to get way out of sight of the Diomede chopper. Far enough to give us a good head start."

Ahead, the low gray coastal mist looked solid, so unyielding that John's heart was in his mouth as Salome plunged straight for it. It enveloped them with terrifying suddenness, and John started back, slamming the window shut on the freezing dampness. Moisture spattered the glass, and Salome fumbled for the controls. The windshield wipers lurched into motion, slapping away huge drops of rain.

"OK, they can't see us," Salome growled. "On the other hand, I can't see *a thing.*"

"You'll fly us into the cliffs!" shouted Slack.

"I have to try!"

John closed his eyes tight. "Stop *yelling.* Stop!"

"What use is—"

"*Shut up!*"

<185>

Slack did. There was no sound but the roar of the engine, the rattle of rotors, and the frantic squeak and slap of the wipers.

For John, it all faded into a distant white noise.

It was as if he were running on some instinctive program; he didn't even reach for his phone. He just clenched his right fist hard.

You're in my flesh. Every instinct, every thought in his head funneled toward that tiny, alien implant. *We have to be compatible. We* are *compatible.*

"John!" Slack's fearful shout was no louder than an irritating buzz.

Permit access, John told the implant. *Now. Access denied.*

Override code, he insisted. *Access required. Identification required.*

Identification NOT required. Override. New code incoming.

ACCESS DENIED.

Override. Override. Over—

DEVICE COMPATIBLE.

John thought for an instant that he was outside the helicopter and falling into the sea. *No.* That was just an illusion. He was tumbling into a green ocean of code and flipping between lines, adjusting, and correcting. No typing necessary. He rewrote the code by instinct, with no more than a thought.

He burst out of his eerie reverie like a diver surfacing. "Give me your hands!"

Snatching Salome's fingers from the central control and grabbing Slack's left hand, he shut his eyes and focused his mind, locking onto the flickering signals that were their implants.

Access granted.

<186>

The code he needed was in his head now: it took only seconds to rewrite it. Slack jolted back as if he'd stuck his finger in a socket; Salome shuddered violently.

"Turn back, Salome," barked John. "Get away from the Russian coastline!"

"Oh God!" screamed Salome, her eyes almost popping out of her head. She wrenched at the control stick between her legs, and John and Slack tumbled back as the helicopter surged upward.

Clutching the door handle, John hauled himself forward, finding his feet. From the left-hand window he saw black solid cliffs veer away from them.

"Close one," he breathed faintly.

"Too close," whispered Salome. She was shaking as she turned the craft, thus leaving the brutal rocks behind them.

"What did you *do*?" demanded Slack as he scrambled to his feet.

"I stopped us from crashing!" she yelled.

"No, not you! John! What did *John just do*?"

"I hacked our implants." John was panting hard. "Reset the trackers inside them. Those choppers think we're over Siberia."

Slack grabbed his arm, swinging him round. His stare was hot with shock and anger. "Never mind what. *How?* What did you hack them *with*?"

John could only shake his head. "Later." Slack stumbled back, and John turned away, unable to meet his eyes. His mental hack of the implants had been automatic, as if the commands had clicked in his head. *I hardly know what I did.*

<187>

As Salome, battling against the wind, moved the craft in a broad circle, John crouched by the window again. She was aiming the nose straight toward the Seward Peninsula now, and it shimmered into sight through a blur of snow and fog.

John tensely watched the coastline grow larger. Streams of fog rushed around the fuselage, the sky was dark, and he hoped Salome's flying skills extended to landing in what looked like miserable weather. He saw her throat jerk as she dived the craft toward the looming fringe of land and realized she was hoping the same.

The heaving sea became frothing waves, then a snow-blanketed claw of land. Salome worked the throttle again, slowing the helicopter, and it swayed violently in the wind. John's stomach lurched with the craft as it lowered far too fast, and he felt a giant jolt as the skids touched the earth. It hopped, slammed down again, and rocked gently.

Salome flicked switches, and the engine died.

Above them, the rotors slowed, quieted, and finally stopped.

Salome slumped forward over the controls, with her fists clenched and her shoulders heaving.

Slack seized her arm. "You are *awesome!* When did you learn to fly a helicopter?"

Her muffled voice trembled. "Never."

"What?" said John.

She flopped back against the pilot seat, pale, her eyes staring. "I can't."

"What do you mean, 'can't'?" Slack hooted. "You were brilliant!"

<188>

"I mean I can't," she yelled, turning on him. "I never learned. I don't know how to fly a helicopter. *I don't know how.*"

The boys stared at her. Slack's gaze darkened as he turned to John and frowned. "So can you explain now—"

"I don't know what Salome's talking about," John interrupted him hurriedly, "but we made it. Now we have to get out of here. Lykos will figure out we're not in Russia, and they'll follow us."

Salome gave an exhausted nod, and between them the two boys dragged the trembling girl from the cockpit.

"Don't think I'm letting this drop," growled Slack over Salome's sagging head as he held her arm. "I want to know how you hacked our implants. You didn't even touch your phone."

John nodded and stretched forward to open the door. An icy blast of pure winter hit them. He flinched, then jumped to the ground.

Salome stumbled down, helped by Slack. "I can't fly. Why could I fly?"

"Never mind," barked John against the howl of the blizzard. "Come on."

He and Slack half carried Salome across a flat expanse of tarmac through driving snow. In the distance, he instantly recognized Wales Airport, but the low buildings were indistinct in the snowy air: Salome had missed the helipad by miles, he realized, and they were on a branch runway far from the center.

Snow and wind buffeted them as they half ran, half stumbled through the blizzard, but John was aware of another creeping sensation. Somewhere deep in his brain, there was a subtle tug.

<189>

Like a cursor, he thought suddenly. *A cursor, blinking away on a blank screen, like it's waiting for something. Like there's an incoming message—*

And, suddenly, text leaped into his mind's eye, flickering through his brain, shining on the inside of his eyelids when he shut his eyes tight.

John. Download waiting . . .

He shook his head violently. He had no idea what was happening—the sudden instinct to hack the implants, the tickle of that waiting cursor in his head—but now was not the time to be distracted.

Ice was forming on his eyelashes, and the gale wind was cold enough to cut into his skin. His chest and throat stung from it.

Download complete.

John almost screamed. *Leave me alone!*

Yet without even thinking about it, he veered ninety degrees. Dragging Salome, he stumbled along a thin strip of snow-covered tarmac, his eyes already seeking what he knew was there.

Shelter. We need to reach it.

"Will someone from the airport come after us?" gasped Slack as he ran.

"They don't know we're here," croaked Salome. "If there's even anyone manning the airport. I received no contact before we landed."

"Eva," rasped John. "I bet she could hide us. Clever . . . clever girl."

They pounded on through the whirling snow flurries. John led them across strips of gravel runway, until at last, in the driving

<190>

gray blast, a low, squat building took shape. With a last surge of energy, he sprinted toward it.

He almost collided with a shabby timber wall. Salome and Slack were right behind him, and the three of them slumped on a stretch of snow-covered grass in the shelter of the little hut. Their panting breaths plumed in the freezing air.

Slack sat doubled up, clutching his knees, gasping. Salome was still shivering, her eyes wide with terror, and nothing would calm her. "I can't fly. *I can't fly.* I don't understand."

"I do," said a new voice.

John leaped to his feet, his heart thundering. *Who was out here?* There was something familiar about the accent, but it wasn't possible. It was in the wrong place. It couldn't be.

A short, round figure materialized in the thick gray air. As it drew closer, it grew into a very slight girl, wrapped in a thick, puffy winter jacket. She wore huge snow boots and a woolen hat that was pulled down to her eyes; her gloved fingers gripped the straps of a bulky backpack. She was just a shape in the driving snow, but John knew her anyway, just by her familiar dark eyes. His heartbeat kicked against his ribs, and he sucked in a shocked breath.

"Hello, John Laine," said Akane. "Nice to meet you at last. I've got a lot to tell you."

<191>

Twenty-Six

The hut had been abandoned long ago. That was obvious now; its dull green paint was peeling, and there were splintered gaps in the wooden boards. John and Slack kicked at the door till it collapsed inward, and then they and Akane helped Salome to her feet. Stumbling forward into the echoing emptiness, they slammed the door shut as best they could, and Slack jammed Akane's huge backpack against it.

For a long time, they sat in silence. John needed to get his breath back even more than the others.

"Akane," he whispered at last. "How did you get here?"

"It doesn't matter how," she said. "What matters is why."

Salome's eyes had begun to regain their fire. "This is your friend from Japan, John?"

"Yes," Akane answered for him. "And it looks like you discovered the same thing I did, or you wouldn't be here."

"We didn't discover anything." Slack leaned forward. "We left because there were men after us. Men with guns. It all started ... because there was a shutdown at the school."

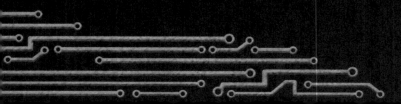

"What happened?"

"A malware infection. Every single device." John stared at Akane, still hardly able to believe she was here. "Reiffelt's up to something bad. All three of us were affected by something in that place—we all had the same nightmares. Killing urges. Then—we discovered Roy Lykos is after us. And that's where the men with guns came in."

"It's worse than I thought," muttered Akane. "Yet I'm not surprised. I was chased too."

"*You?* They came after you? Why?" John rubbed at his temples with his fingernails. "Someone had been warning me, telling me to get out." He hesitated. "Was that you, Akane?"

She shook her head. "No, that wasn't me."

He looked at her intently. "But you did message me. On my broken phone."

She glanced up, biting her lip as if she were tormented. "Yes. I did."

"*How?*"

Slack was looking from John to Akane, his eyes narrow. "You mean, like you hacked our implants with nothing but your head?"

Akane glanced at him. "Did you, John? That was clever."

"Somebody had better start explaining themselves." Salome spoke through chattering teeth, but her voice was determined.

"*Two* people, in fact," muttered Slack.

Akane let out a deep breath. "A year ago," she said, "John found files of mine that he shouldn't have been able to find. I don't mean it was hard—I mean it was *impossible*. And he did it by downloading a key. He didn't do that with a computer. He did it with instinct. Downloaded it straight into his head. As if *he* were the device." They stared at her.

<193>

"You can't hack with your *instincts*," snapped Salome. She sounded more frightened than angry. "With your *head*."

"It was just luck," said John hoarsely.

"No. It wasn't." Akane peeled off her wet gloves and shook her hair free of her beanie. "I've been hunting for an explanation ever since then, John. It's driven me crazy. But it wasn't till you went to the Center that I found the answer. And *that* was a coincidence, or luck, if you like. Because when I broke into the Wolf's Den files, I wasn't expecting to solve the puzzle of *you*." She swallowed hard. "But I did."

"So *how*?" John clenched his fists. "How did I do it?"

"Last year you were struggling to find a way into my files. And your programming knew where to find the answer. In the Cloud."

"Don't be crazy," he laughed. "You wouldn't have stored your key in—"

"The Cloud that exists between us." Akane spoke over him. "Just us. Our personal, linked storage, the Cloud that only we have access to. Your programming kicked in and downloaded it."

There was a heavy silence. "His programming . . ." echoed Salome.

"And yours, Salome. And Slack's." Akane unzipped her jacket and drew out her phone.

She tapped the screen and turned it to face them. "I've been doing some hacking."

"Scorpion's gonna sting," said John.

She didn't smile as she usually would, and he frowned at the phone as she handed it to him. Salome and Slack looked over his shoulder as he scrolled through Akane's bookmarked pages. His eyes widened.

<194>

"Here's the thing," she told them quietly. "We all had accidents when we were little. Bad accidents. I fell off a temple roof and broke my skull." She touched something on the back of her head. "John tried to climb on rocks, and he fell too; he nearly died. Jake—Slack—was in a boating accident; the boom knocked him overboard, and he was trapped under the keel. You drowned, Slack. You were dead."

Slack blinked at her. "I . . . know."

"And Salome? You got away from your nanny. You ran into a road in Lagos and were hit by a high-speed car."

"Is that true?" John turned to her. Salome nodded wordlessly.

"There was only one man who could save us." Akane turned to John. "Mikael Laine."

There was silence.

"Now." Akane leaned over and tapped on her phone screen. "We actually weren't treatable, none of us. We were effectively dead. We *should* have died. But your dad, John—he was developing a new technique. He was combining genetically altered DNA with a form of artificial intelligence—one with biological adaptations. He was trying to merge the two seamlessly. And I don't think it was quite ready. I don't think he'd perfected it yet. He wouldn't have used it, maybe not for years. But then, John—you had your accident."

"And he experimented on his own son," whispered Salome, "because otherwise he'd have lost him. It was his last resort."

"I guess it worked." Akane shrugged. "Because he started using it on more patients. He used it on the three of us."

"Artificial intelligence." John's blood seemed to have slowed to a cold, sluggish trickle. "I've got AI in my system?"

Akane cleared her throat. "We all do."

<195>

John stared down at his fist. The knuckles were white. "What does it do? I mean—what's the point?"

"The point is it kept us alive," murmured Akane. "But, yes, there was a method to his madness." She glanced quickly at John. "I don't mean he was crazy. But there had to be some kind of madness in the things he was doing. Who else would have thought of this, let alone tried it?"

"My dad," whispered John hoarsely, "he wouldn't do something evil."

"He didn't think it was evil." Akane grasped his hand. "*I* don't think it is either. It is what it is. John, let me ask you something. Do you ever *feel* like . . . like a computer?"

He swallowed hard. "John is the computer."

"Exactly. And so am I. So are all of us. Sometimes I get sort of . . . taken over. Like a program's running in the background and I'm barely there at all. I'm just following prompts, you know?"

John nodded. His brain felt heavy. "It happened at the Center. When I was working on the malware. In class. Even when we did those aptitude tests, right at the start . . . "

"I've felt it before too," said Slack. "But never as *strongly* as I did at the Center."

Salome cleared her throat. "It's like . . . flying."

"Or diving into a strong current," said Slack. "And letting it carry you along."

"But the thing is this technology is decades ahead of its time. When I studied the files, at first I thought I was crazy. But I tried it out. I thought: what if I wanted to download information *into me?* Not my device—*me.* I picked something I never even tried, never even thought of trying: analyzing the cellular structure of Otou-

<196>

chan's spider plant. I held a leaf in my hands, and I meditated. I wrote down the information . . . " She shrugged. "And then I looked it up on an academic botanical site. And I was right. *Exactly* right."

"But my phone . . . " began John. "How did you . . . "

"Yes, I also tried *uploading* from my head. It took a lot of practice and a lot of meditation, but at last everything just clicked. I accessed your phone *with my mind.* Or rather, with the AI genetic material inside my brain. I've never *heard* of tech like that." She shrugged. "Can you imagine what it's worth?"

"Roy Lykos," rasped John. "That's why he was after us."

"I saw his name in the files," murmured Akane. "He was using the code name Freki."

The familiarity of it clicked suddenly, the name the gunman had called Lykos. "Freki was one of Odin's wolves," said John slowly.

"So I discovered. That's how I finally made the connection with the Wolf's Den—and then I tracked the code name to Lykos. Yasuo Yamamoto signed the contracts, but it was Roy who masterminded everything."

"Yasuo is the one with the money," murmured Salome. "He financed the Wolf's Den."

"I saw his name on contracts," nodded Akane. "Roy Lykos was involved in the development of the modified DNA," she went on, "but he didn't make the breakthrough—his colleague did. *Your dad*, John. You should have seen some of Lykos's emails to him. So cold and bitter. And *jealous*."

"Roy hinted that he'd met Dad," rasped John. "He didn't say he'd *worked* with him for years."

<197>

"Lykos wants us in his hands," said Salome calmly. "Roy and Yasuo and Ms. Reiffelt. They want this technology."

"And they're going to keep coming after us," said Akane grimly. "They're not going to stop. John, that feeling, that out-of-body sensation—I thought it was just the way I was. I thought that was how *everybody* felt when they got onto a computer. But it's not. It's just me, and you, and us." She nodded at Slack and Salome. "Because it's in our DNA."

Salome jerked up, as if a current had run through her bones. "The helicopter—"

"You said afterward you couldn't fly one," said Slack.

"Ah." Akane bit her lip. "Like my spider plant. See, the tech doesn't just make us great coders and hackers. Salome, your programming accessed the ability to *fly a helicopter*. For as long as you needed to do it. Could you get into that chopper right now and fly us to Anchorage?"

Salome recoiled. "No," she said with a shaky smile. "Keep that thing away from me!"

"Then . . ." Akane looked as if she was running through thousands of files in her head; *maybe she is*, realized John. "The AI inside you—it knows you're safe for now. So the data will delete itself, to make room for more information if you need it." Her brow furrowed. "Hang on . . ."

She leaned over to tap the screen again. John's eyes flickered down the data and the graphs, assimilating it in an instant. *That's how it works. Yes, the storage will cope with that many terabytes of data but then—*

He quickly shifted his eyes toward Akane's. "I just did it again!"

"Yep. Your drive's making space for the information."

<198>

"This is *awesome!*" yelled Slack, jumping to his feet. "We're cyborgs!"

John couldn't share his excitement. A dull gloom was creeping over him. "I thought it was me. That only I was *talented*. I thought I was good at this stuff."

Akane shook his arm. "It *is* you, John."

He couldn't help feeling it wasn't. "It looks like Eva's the only one of us who's really smart. Naturally smart, I mean."

"Ah." Akane took the phone. "I've got a theory about that. When you mentioned Eva, John, I started searching the medical records for her too. I couldn't find any data at all. Not a single file—not even a school one."

"That ties in with everything else about her," sighed Salome. "What's your theory?"

"I think . . . " Akane stared at her screen. "Mikael's early records do talk about other subjects. Experiments that . . . didn't quite pan out." She raised her eyes. "I think Eva Vygotsky's one of them."

"The faulty one," John whispered. "That's what Lykos called her."

"The teachers are wary around her," said Salome. "She's so odd. Imogen Black's suspicious of her. Yasuo avoids her. Roy actively dislikes her."

"Remember what Eva said when she found the malware?" John rubbed his arms, shivering. "She said if she couldn't fix it, she'd lose her whole mind."

"I thought she was being overly dramatic," said Salome, drawing her hands down her face. "Maybe . . . she meant it literally."

"Because she knew instinctively it could infect *her*." John felt sick. "If it can delete the Wolf's Den files and her brain is practically digital . . . what could it do to her?"

<199>

"Delete . . . " whispered Salome.

They sat for a long moment, with horror sinking over them like a heavy, dark cloud.

"Do you think she knows?" asked Slack suddenly.

"She may not know for sure, but I bet she *suspects*. She has those strange episodes, like she switches off." Salome sighed. "I used to joke that she might be a robot—not that she laughed. If Akane got to the bottom of this," she said firmly, "Eva definitely could."

"We have to get her out of that Center," said John desperately.

"Oh, *no*." Salome's eyes widened as she clutched her braids. "I let her stay there. I *let her stay* on that island. You tried to persuade her to come with us, John. But I was so obsessed by the helicopter, it was all I could think about. I didn't even try to—"

"Your programming," John reassured her. "The data was taking up all your bytes."

"That's right." Akane nodded. "It wasn't you, Salome, so don't feel guilty."

Slack stood up, propping himself against the ramshackle wall. "But what does the Center have to do with all this?"

"John's father was one of the founding directors of the Wolf's Den." Akane turned the phone toward John. "He set it up with Roy Lykos specifically for the development of this project. I've read so many files. I've read email threads between them that go on for *volumes*. They were close, John—until you had your accident and your Dad was forced to make that breakthrough. And Lykos got too greedy too soon."

Roy's lies tumbled through John's mind, and his head began to ache. "It looks like my dad always meant for me to go to the Center. He changed his plans because of Lykos."

<200>

"I reckon Mikael almost *created* the Wolf's Den for you," said Akane. "To keep you safe, as well as further his work." She sighed. "But then he discovered Roy's motives, and they weren't good. That's when he vanished."

John's voice rasped in his throat. "Did Lykos kill him?"

"I don't know," said Akane bleakly. She touched his hand. "But your dad did love you, John. It's why he did this *thing* to you in the first place."

"Flies and honey," whispered John. "With Dad out of the way, Lykos used the Center to attract us and keep us."

"So why the malware attack?" demanded Slack.

"I don't know." Akane sighed. "A distraction? I don't think it was Lykos's doing."

"The Russians?" suggested Slack.

Salome shrugged. "It could have been any regime. Or any private organization that wanted the tech."

"So," said Slack, "the Wolf's Den people weren't the only ones who were after us."

"More importantly, what do we do *now*?" Salome spread her hands. "Where do we go?"

"Far from the Wolf's Den," said Akane. "You shouldn't go back there."

"Not while Lykos is the alpha wolf," said John bitterly. The sting of betrayal was sharp. "He's taken over my dad's whole project."

"The Center isn't bad in itself, I think," murmured Akane. "After all, like John says, it's his dad's creation. But we all have to stay away from it now."

"But we can't go home," Slack pointed out grimly. "They'd just come for us there!"

<201>

"For sure," Akane nodded. "They came for me in Tokyo."

"And we can't trust anyone around here," said Salome. "Those helicopters took off from this airport. If we ask for help, they could turn us straight over to the hunters."

They stared at one another in silence.

At that moment, a green light shone with sudden intensity from Akane's phone. Alarmed, she lifted it.

"Those are coordinates." Salome eyed the digits pulsing on the screen.

"And I didn't put them there." Akane gave a reluctant grin. "I've been hacked."

65 33 31 N

167 56 53 W

"That's all it says?" Salome winced. "Anyone could have sent that."

"We'll ignore it." John shuddered.

"No." Akane's voice was hoarse as she pointed at the screen. "John."

John is on the computer

The now-familiar cursor flickered again.

John is the computer

John's heart was in his throat. He could barely speak the word. "*Dad?*"

John is the computer. Leona is the bug.

65 33 31 N

167 56 53 W

John's eyes were hot. "Dad," he whispered again.

"John," whispered Salome. "John, are you serious?"

"We can't trust that!" exclaimed Slack.

<202>

"Yes. Yes, we can." John raised his eyes. "It was our joke, me and Dad. *Just* us. We used to laugh about Leona always borrowing my computer. It drove me crazy. I got so angry, but Dad would laugh. He said it was a bug in the system. But we never shared that with anyone. Because it would have hurt Leona's feelings. And Mom's." He was hoarse now, his throat thick with tears. "We never told a soul. *It was just us.*"

Akane leaned over to hug John—but her phone crackled so loudly that she yelped, jerked back, and almost dropped it.

"Listen to me."

John flung himself forward, grabbing the phone from Akane. "Dad? *Dad!*" The screen was a blizzard of static, the face an unidentifiable fuzz of green light, but he knew that voice. "DAD!"

"Listen, all of you. Please."

John was too choked up to respond.

"I don't have much time." The blurred, streaked shape glanced nervously over its shoulder. "Akane's figured out so much, but you need details. I don't know how long this connection will stay up. Or unmonitored."

"We're listening," John rasped.

"The DNA in your bodies: it's true. It's genetically modified and spliced with a form of AI, but there's more. You're all—each one of you—connected to a network of supercomputers. The Wolf's Den is part of that network, but it's not the heart of it. Remember the key lines in some of your favorite stories, John?" A smile crept into the crackling voice; John could hear it, and he blinked hard. "Magic is strong at the conjunction of those key lines. And that's like the Wolf's Den."

<203>

"But you said it's not the heart of the network," Salome interrupted sharply.

"No. That's IIDA. That's what I called her, the mainframe supercomputer."

Her. His father was talking as if IIDA was a person, thought John. "She triggered our . . . abilities?"

"Not triggered. You've all had your abilities since I operated on you—but at the Wolf's Den nexus, you got a massive signal boost from IIDA, through the network. The work you've been doing there has given you access to IIDA. She recognized you and synchronized with you."

"That's freaky," murmured Slack, but he didn't sound freaked out. He sounded impressed.

"John, you received messages while you were at the Center. They came from IIDA. She recognized danger and prompted you to get out."

"Because you created her." John's eyes burned, and he gritted his teeth to stop himself from crying. "She wanted us somewhere safe."

"Yes. She did. And so do I, but you're not safe, not yet. And I know Akane has a way to get you out, but she can't do it here."

"You *know*?" Akane grabbed the phone back from John.

"IIDA is my baby, Akane. Of course I know."

They all fell silent. The image on the phone screen jittered and frazzled.

"I'm sorry. All of you. I had no choice but to operate. You were dead."

Slack licked his lips and swallowed. "We understand." He seemed to speak for all of them; they nodded to each other.

<204>

"The tech wasn't ready, but I had to make it ready. I had to bring you back from the grave." There might have been a smile in the crackling voice. "That's why you're my Ghost Network."

"Ghost Network," said Slack, the corner of his lip twitching. "I like it."

"Now go to the coordinates I sent you. This connection is about to be dropped. Goodbye, my ghosts."

"Dad." John seized the phone again. "Dad!"

The screen was blank, as dead as he'd thought his father was. He stared at it for a long time anyway, not trusting himself to look up.

Akane was tapping rapidly on her phone, her intense expression lit by the glow of the screen. At last, she pointed toward the southeast.

"OK, I googled it. Cape Mountain is that way, and beyond it . . . these coordinates are for a place called Tin City. On the mainland, south of here."

"City?" Slack brightened.

"Don't get excited," she told him dryly. "It's less of a city than the one on Diomede. It's a long-range radar station, abandoned by the USAF. There's a ground support station and a military airstrip—that's all."

"And how is that supposed to help us?" asked John. He cleared his throat and gritted his teeth. *Dad's alive. This is all insane.*

"I don't know." Akane shrugged. "But these are the only instructions we're going to get, and they're not just from Mikael. You know what my programming's telling me?"

She gazed at them all, her mouth curling slightly.

"IIDA agrees with Mikael. We're going to Tin City."

<205>

Twenty-Seven

"There's a path that way." Akane's voice was muffled by her thick hood. "But it's longer and too obvious, and I don't think we should take it. I think we should head cross-country, across the flank of the mountain."

"In this weather?" squeaked Salome. She peered into the blinding blizzard toward the lowest visible slopes. Most of Cape Mountain, including its summit, was hidden in icy cloud cover.

"I'm fine with that." Slack pulled an extra woolen beanie over the one Eva had given him. Akane's bulging backpack had been stuffed with winter clothing, along with dried survival rations, glow sticks, hand warmers, and even a folding shovel.

"I couldn't carry tents," she explained. "We'll have to dig a snow shelter if we get in trouble."

"No problem." Slack looked almost cheerful. "Been there, done that."

"Our footwear is the only problem," said John darkly. "But according to the map on Akane's phone, it's only about five miles to the radar station. We can last that long. Surely." He glanced doubtfully at Salome's thin boots.

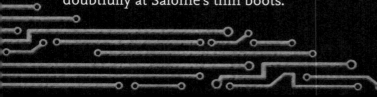

"I suggest," said Salome briskly, "we stop talking and get walking."

And, as always, when Salome gave instructions, they found themselves obeying.

<<>>

An easterly wind bit their faces as they trudged through the blizzard, with Slack taking the lead with Akane's compass. They were already high above sea level, and the slope kept rising. John could feel frost crystals forming on his eyelashes, dragging his eyelids down; he dreaded to think how bad it would get at a higher altitude. *Five miles, that's all.*

Yeah. Five miles across the worst terrain I've ever seen. In an Arctic blizzard.

It was going to take focus, and he was struggling to find that. The contact from Mikael still seemed like a dream, an illusion. But in his gut, he knew it was real. *And Dad thinks we can make it to Tin City. That means we can.*

Gritting his teeth, John walked.

Nobody wanted to waste energy on conversation. They'd been trudging in weary silence for more than an hour when Akane dropped back to walk at his side. John could hear her harsh panting breaths. *And she's in better shape than any of us.*

"I know you've got a lot to process," she said through her chattering teeth.

"You're not kidding." He tried to smile, but his face felt frozen.

"Do you have doubts, John?"

He gave her a wry glance. "Of course I do. But it's all true. My programming says so."

<207>

"IIDA," she muttered.

"Why did he go away, Akane? Why did he let us think he was dead?"

She halted, her breath pluming like smoke. "I don't know, John. But he had his reasons. Look at what Lykos tried to do. Your dad knew what he was."

John nodded, then hitched his pack higher on his shoulders. "Come on. The blizzard's getting stronger."

Taking the hint, Akane fell silent as they struggled on through the deepening drifts.

"Your sister is the best," she panted after a while.

"I . . . know." The shock of Akane's story could still take John's mind off his aching chest and his already-wet feet. "What's the plan? Where is she now?"

"In Nome. With Brody and the others. She thinks I caught a boat ride to Diomede, but I couldn't get one. So I waited. At the airport. We can"—Akane sucked in a harsh breath—"contact her by phone. That's what your dad knew. I'll tell her to get the plane to the airstrip at Tin City. Pick us up and fly us back to Nome."

"It's a plan," said John doubtfully.

"It's our only plan." She plodded grimly on.

Ahead of John, Salome was stumbling in the deepening snow. He picked up his pace, anxious.

"You OK?"

She could only nod. "Done worse."

"Liar." John managed a grin.

The mountain's flank rose before them, smooth and white beneath a looming charcoal sky. The hope that surged as they approached each false summit was followed by a crushing

<208>

despair as another upward stretch was revealed. *One foot in front of the other. One foot in front—*

Salome gave a hoarse cry as she stumbled forward. John crouched and hauled her to her feet.

"I don't think I can do this," she whispered.

"Come on," he urged her through his frozen lips. "All that gym time!"

"It's the cold," she mumbled. "My feet. They're soaking."

Great clumps of snow had stuck to the soles of her boots. John knocked the ice away as best he could with his gloved fist.

"You have to keep going," he muttered. "Come on, Salome." He dragged her forward, and with a groan she stumbled on.

Without Slack, he thought, they wouldn't have gotten even this far. His friend seemed to know exactly what he was doing, adjusting their course by small increments, forging upward but keeping the sea to their right and the steep incline to the summit on their left. John couldn't see the ocean through the murky air, but he could hear it, a low distant booming at the foot of the mountain's western slopes. From time to time Slack glanced skyward, seeming frustrated. *I bet he'd be navigating by the sun and the stars if he could see them,* thought John. There was more to his friend than he'd realized.

But five miles seemed like forever.

Salome was leaning heavily on his arm now, her trudging steps an automatic force of habit. She could hardly lift her feet; she left a dragging trench through the snow as each boot lurched forward.

I don't know how much longer she can go on, John thought with a stab of dull panic. *We have to rest again. Just for a moment.*

<209>

No, we can't. Every time they did, he was afraid Salome would never be able to start walking again. But the pain in his lungs and muscles was acute, and his legs were failing. Against his will, he stumbled to a halt, sagging against the exhausted Salome.

John raised his head to shout to Slack, and the words froze in his throat.

Slack had already stopped. He turned, and the grim, dogged despair had left his face. Light gleamed on his grinning teeth.

John blinked painfully. *Light. Snow light. Sunlight.*

The dragging blanket of clouds was lifting as he watched. The force of the blizzard had faltered, and slits of blue had appeared among the solid looming gray.

And the summit was visible.

This time, John knew it was for real: a perfect, unnatural sphere perched at the summit's crest, high up to their left. The white globe glittered in the sun's rays; below it, a row of pylons marched down the slope and disappeared over a low ridge. They too were completely white, iced over with snow.

"The radar station!" barked Slack. "We're nearly there!"

John's frozen face cracked into a smile. "It's downhill from here!" he told Salome hoarsely. "Come on. You can do this!"

Her muscles stiffened, she took a sharp breath, and faintly he heard her croak, "Yes."

With a crunch of snow, Akane appeared at his side. Her eyes were all he could see behind her hood and tightly wrapped face, and they were furrowed with concern. "Salome needs to rest for a bit. Eat something." She crouched to rummage in her backpack for an energy bar.

<210>

Slack forged on for another hundred yards or so, scoping out the downward incline, and John struggled through the knee-deep snow to his side.

His friend turned, his expression ominous.

"You know how you're scared of heights, John?"

<<>>

The four of them stood on the edge of the precipice and peered at the ground far below.

"I've gotten down steeper slopes," said Akane. "But what about Salome? Are you up for it?"

Salome shot her a dry look. She looked re-energized: maybe by the food, maybe by the clear sky, maybe simply by the prospect of the journey being almost over. "I'm not walking farther than I have to," she growled. "This is the quickest way to the base station, and I'm taking it. It's like the climbing wall at the Wolf's Den."

"But real," groaned John, taking a step back. His stomach lurched, and his head swam.

"If we don't go this way, we'll have a detour of several miles," Salome told him sternly. "You told me I could cross the mountain, and I did. Now it's my turn to tell you. You're capable of this, John. You know the basics from the Center."

"This isn't a climbing wall." He shivered. "It's a full-on deadly cliff. And I think I got *nineteen feet* up the climbing wall. I'm a beginner!"

Akane placed a hand on his arm. "It's not vertical. We don't need rappelling gear. Just take it slow."

"*How?*"

"Think," she murmured. "Or—no. Don't think. Let IIDA do your thinking. Remember everything I've told you about meditating, John? It's no time for a crash course. But try."

John wished she hadn't used the words "crash course." But he obeyed her as he stepped back from the edge and closed his eyes. He took several deep breaths to slow his thumping heartbeat.

It happened faster than he could have imagined. Like an emergency protocol, something at the back of his brain snapped into life. *Holds. Grabs.*

He panted, startled, and his eyes snapped open. *Again. I need more information!*

Rock temperature: adjust for conditions. Ice tension. Adapt. Make allowances. This is how.

He closed his eyes and it scrolled down the inside of his eyelids like lines of code, but a code he could read like a child's storybook. *This is how. No need to learn. You know it.*

I know it.

He slowly blinked his eyes open and flexed his fingers. "Can we go now? I'm afraid I'll forget."

"You won't forget." Akane gazed into his eyes. "Pass the knowledge into your cells. Your body will do the rest." She grinned. "There is no *try*, padawan. There is only *do*."

John turned awkwardly, lowered himself over the edge, and began the descent.

<<>>

Later, John couldn't even remember how he'd done it. It was as if Parallel John were making the climb, and he was simply along for the ride. One foothold, one handhold to the next,

<212>

he climbed steadily downward, his brain guiding his limbs, making adjustments, signaling warnings. *That blade of rock isn't safe.* He moved his hand. *The ice has loosened the scree to your left. Avoid that patch; the ice is bad.*

He was barely aware of the others; he was moving faster than all of them. The wall of stone in front of his eyes might as well have been a screen: information flickered across it, guiding and directing. Climbing down was like scrolling the screen, and its flickering data was constant—

Except when it stopped.

And his feet were firmly on the gravelly ground.

And when he turned, blinking the program away, he saw only a broad sweep of icy plain and the frozen sea beyond. And between them, in the near distance, lay the cluster of abandoned huts that was Tin City.

<213>

Twenty-Eight

"I told you so," said Akane smugly.

John grinned. "You did."

The four of them huddled in one of the abandoned huts as the wind howled and rattled the iron roof above them. Slack had thrown safety to the winds and lit Akane's tiny gas-canister stove. He'd perched it beneath a cracked-open window, in a gesture to not give them carbon monoxide poisoning, so he could boil dried food packets in melted snow.

Akane tapped intently at her phone, but she couldn't keep the smile of achievement off her face. "I can't believe we made it. And we didn't die."

"*We* didn't really make it, did we?" John made a face. He'd always thought of himself as clever—preternaturally clever—and he'd been proud of it. It wasn't as if he was good at sports or English lit; computer science had been his special talent. But it sounded like he'd got the *preternaturally* part right, if nothing else.

And it all comes back to Dad. He's the one who did this to me.

To relieve his feelings, he kicked at a broken desk. "It was the programming. It was IIDA."

Akane tilted her head. "IIDA gave us information; all we had to do was access it. She's like our mom sending us stern text messages. But John—we're the ones who have to rise to the challenge."

"Our Mom." John managed to laugh. *Three mothers.* That was what he'd blurted to Salome and Slack, back at the Center: Tina, Salome, and . . . *Yeah, that was how it felt. Hi, other-other Mom. Thanks for nothing.*

And you, Dad. Relief and affection warred with bitter resentment.

"I got through to Leona and Brody and the others," Akane interrupted, clicking her phone off. "They're heading here in a couple of hours. Leona just has a bit of shopping to finish."

"In Nome?" John gave a bark of laughter. "My sister could find a Macy's in the Sahara."

"As long as they've got an internet café, I'll be happy." There was a mischievous glint in Akane's eyes. "There's one way we can help Eva. I've got an idea about that malware."

"I thought you might. Thanks for coming all this way, Akane." John grew serious. "We wouldn't have made it out without you."

"We haven't *quite* made it yet," Akane warned him.

"You think the hunters might track us down here?" asked John nervously. He glanced around, half expecting black-clad figures to swing through shattered windows while toting automatic rifles. "I mean, we're sitting ducks if they find out where we've gone."

<215>

"Yes. But the Center's still locked down. Nobody's tracking this phone—I've made sure of it—and yours is lifeless again. With luck, those gunmen will expect us to stay around Wales. They're probably searching every cranny of it now. Ha."

"Sloppy joes and chili tacos all round," yelled Slack from the stove. "Well, it's . . . " he peered at the empty packets, "curried chicken stew, and it looks revolting, but it's food."

They lingered over the meal while wrinkling their noses at the chewy lumps of chicken, but they enjoyed hot food at last.

"I guess we're still human enough to be hungry," said Slack with a wry grin.

"I've been thinking." John set his bowl aside. "Dad said that when we were at the Center, we synced in some way with this supercomputer, this IIDA?"

Akane nodded. "I guess the longer you were there, the harder you worked and used your brains and the faster the connection became."

"But the nightmares," said John darkly. "We all had them. Those could only have come from IIDA."

"Waking nightmares," Slack reminded him. He looked as if he'd suddenly lost his appetite. "I don't think a powerful urge to kill two people is a very benevolent sort of program."

Salome put her bowl down. "Are we *for* something?" she asked. "Because I want to make a positive difference in the world. I don't want to be used to kill anyone."

"I don't want to be used at all," said Slack.

Akane chewed thoughtfully; she was the only one still eating. "I think we are *for* something, yes. Or we *could* be used. Why else

<216>

would Lykos want to get his hands on us? Why would your principal say she had the 'subjects secure'?"

John shivered.

"But the dreams," Akane went on. "These kids, this Leo and Adam—you suspect they installed the malware, right? I don't think IIDA wanted you to *kill* them. I think your programs just wanted you to delete the bug. That's all."

Delete. That was the word his brain had used. John brightened.

"It wasn't an instruction." Akane shrugged. "It was an electronic instinct."

"That makes sense," said Slack. A happy grin began to form on his face. "It really does. Hey, I'm not a homicidal maniac!" He paused, considering. "John probably is, though."

John growled and smacked his shoulder with a glove.

"So you weren't *created* to do bad thi—" Akane stopped, tilting her head.

John held his breath. Distantly, from the sky beyond the hut, came the faint sound of a twin-prop engine.

"John," smiled Akane, getting to her feet. "I do believe your sister finished her shopping early."

<217>

Twenty-Nine

"Ye of little faith," said Slack, leaning back on his plastic chair. "I told you Nome would have an internet café."

"Sh," said Akane. "I'm concentrating."

"Did you get into the North West Campus's system?" John craned eagerly over her shoulder.

"Yup." Akane looked satisfied. "Their encryption algorithms were pathetic. The Wolf's Den may be Digital Fort Knox, but I've got half of Alaska University's capacity working for me now."

"I hope it's working fast," said Salome. "Leona and her friends said they wanted to leave for Anchorage well before sundown. They'll be back to pick us up any minute."

"We've almost done it." John turned back to his own keyboard. "Akane was right—there is a back door to the Wolf's Den. I caught a glimpse of it before—I bet that's what triggered the full takeover by the malware. Adam and Leo said something—that I just got too close for comfort." He furrowed his brow and focused on the café computer. "But all the bad guys' digital fire is concentrated on keeping out the tech staff on Diomede. They're

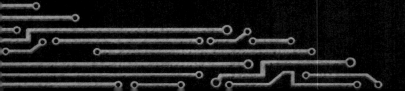

not watching over their shoulders for some internet café in Nome. Look—see that oscillating variable matrix?" He jabbed at his screen. "That's the hacker's footprint, right there."

Salome whistled. "Clever. And sneaky."

"And not Adam and Leo," added John. "They might have installed the malware, but they didn't create it. They were acting under orders."

"And we can guess whose," murmured Salome.

"Ten minutes," growled Akane. "That's all I need." She glared at the virus as if she wanted to throttle it with its own digital trail.

She'd said ten minutes; between them, they were done in six. John gave a bark of triumph and shoved his chair back on its casters, spinning till he almost hit the wall.

"Bang, bang, Velociraptor. You are *dead*."

They exchanged whoops and fist bumps, drawing perplexed stares from the café owners and the scattering of patrons.

Salome became subdued and thoughtful. "I'm glad we did this. We owed it to Eva."

John nodded. "She's still in danger, but at least her mind will be intact."

"Yes." A voice crackled from the screen.

"*Dad?*" John scooted his chair back to the computer, and the others clustered in a huddle around him. There was no blizzard of pixels this time, no sign of Mikael at all: only an old and slightly blurred photo. Eva Vygotsky stood against sunlight that made a white halo around her pale hair. Her black-rimmed eyes were clear and penetrating.

"My mistake. My fault. Not hers. Thank you for helping her."

<219>

"It's not enough," blurted Salome. "We can't just leave Eva there, Mikael."

"You must not return to the Wolf's Den. Not now. But we'll find a way to help her, I promise."

"Dad." John leaned closer, staring hard. "How could you do all this? *Why* did you do it? To Eva, to us?"

"For you, John. You know that." The voice halted for a moment. "I went too far. I know that. Remember Icarus, John? I flew too close to the sun."

The photo of Eva dissolved, replaced by that static-blurred figure, and the voice was firm and dispassionate once again.

"He's on his way. You have time, but it's measured in hours."

"Lykos?" Slack crouched over the screen.

"He won't give you up, not that easily. He's at Wales Airport now."

Salome looked as if she wanted to cry. Instead, she raged. "So we move *again*. Where are we supposed to hide from him?"

"I'm sending you new coordinates. First you have to get to Anchorage, but do not return to Fairbanks. Not under any circumstances. Akane, you can't go back to Tokyo."

"No," she agreed softly, "I understand that. They already tracked me down there."

"I'll contact you all again in Anchorage, let you know where to go from there. A safe place. There's so much you can do: so much that's good, that can benefit the whole world. But you could be used for evil; it's why I ran, John. That and the fact Lykos would have killed me."

"I know." John nodded reluctantly.

<220>

"I hoped to protect you by faking my own death; instead, I left you vulnerable. There are people at the Wolf's Den who could manipulate you into something terrible. Understand this, my young ghosts: you must not be caught. You're too strong and too untrained. Lykos must not have you."

"We understand," said Slack grimly.

"There are others like you, in centers like the Wolf's Den, all over the world. It's not just Eva. And not all of them are 'faulty.'"

"Others?" blurted Akane eagerly.

"Together we can save Eva. But right now you need to get far away from the Wolf's Den. You have work to do, and so do I. I will see you in person—" For a moment, the strong voice faltered.

John's breath caught in his throat. Resentment, anger, relief, joy: he didn't know which was the strongest. The fuzzy on-screen image seemed to resolve a little, and eyes were almost visible: blue and clear and staring right into his.

"I promise you, John. Soon."

The image flickered, dissolved into streaks, and faded to blankness.

John watched as the innocuous internet café login popped back up. It took him a few long seconds to realize that his friends were all staring at him.

"Are you OK, John?" Slack touched his shoulder.

"I'm fine." For the first time in ages, John realized, it was true. He took a deep breath. "Are we all doing this, then? Going on the run? Hiding from a supervillain?"

"You bet!" Slack grinned. "But you forgot 'training ourselves to be the best white-hat hackers in the world'!"

<221>

He and Akane shared a fist bump, but Salome looked subdued. "Of course we're all running. We have no choice."

"I'll tell my parents I won a scholarship, that I'm staying here." Akane shrugged wryly. "It'll take some explaining, but I'll find an excuse to stay away from home for a while. I can't put my family in danger."

"We'll be in danger ourselves," warned Salome.

"Danger is my middle name," smiled Akane. "We're in this together."

"All for one, and one for all." John couldn't help laughing.

"Excellent!" Slack's blue eyes glinted. "Long live the Ghost Network!"

"Let's get out of here." Grinning, John picked up his bag, but as a flicker caught his eye, he froze, and he turned slowly back to the screen.

His pulse thumped in his throat. He clicked on the box. *Log in.*

Luminous green type flashed onto a plain black screen.

>HELP

Chills shivered across John's skin. He leaned down, typing so fast he was clumsy.

Ddad? E/va? Who r you?

>HELP ME

The pause as the cursor blinked was agonizingly long, and then letters appeared again, halting and jerky.

>WOLVES

And the screen went dead.

<222>

Next page loading . . .

Look for these books!

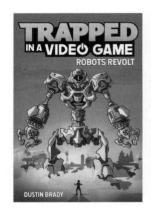